Smiles on Washington Square

SMILES ON WASHINGTON SQUARE

(A LOVE STORY OF SORTS)

Raymond Federman

NEW YORK

Copyright © 1985 by Raymond Federman

All rights reserved

Published in the United States by

Thunder's Mouth Press, Box 780, New York, NY 10025

Design by Loretta Li

Grateful acknowledgment is made to the

New York State Council on the Arts and

the National Endowment for the Arts

for financial assistance.

Library of Congress Cataloging in Publication Data

Federman, Raymond.   Smiles on Washington Square.

I. Title.

PS3556.E25S6   1985   813'.54   85-7939

ISBN 0-938410-29-6

Distributed by

PERSEA BOOKS, Inc.

225 Lafayette Street, New York, NY 10012

(212) 431-5270

For George Chambers
and all the vain repetitions

It rained for four years,
eleven months, and two days.

—GABRIEL GARCIA MARQUEZ
One Hundred Years of Solitude

Smiles on Washington Square

O N E

The story of Moinous & Sucette.
Their love story. It should be told.
The intensity of its hope. The fury of its
conditional disappointment. It should be told,
one way or another. They first meet in New York,
one afternoon in March. Or perhaps in February. Nothing
unusual. Well almost meet, when they are both in the
same place at the same time. But that day they do not
speak. No. They smile at each other, nothing more. A fleet-
ing, complicitous smile, as if they know they are destined
to meet again.

Reason enough to mention this initial encounter across
a smile, even though Moinous & Sucette do not really
speak that day. But they do come face to face, and that
should be noted; for later, when they reach the peak of
their passionate relationship, they will often recall that
twinkle of recognition, that impromptu eye-to-eye contact,
and the smiles they exchanged as a sign of a future conniv-
ance. Not that it is love at first sight. The classic thunder-
bolt of love. That would be too banal. But they immediately sense in that quick mutual exchange of smiles a
potential emotional affinity. And that's good enough to get
things started, especially since they are both lonely that
day and in need of human fellowship.

Let's say that it is Tuesday the first time they meet. Almost meet. And let's say that it is raining. Cats and dogs,
for the sake of the mood. What the hell, it always rains in
sad love stories. And in happy ones too. Must be a reason,
though not necessarily metaphysical. And let's say that

3

they meet in the street. Somewhere in the streets of New York City, way downtown.

Washington Square. Yes that's where they come face to face for the first time when they accidentally bump into each other and smile. A pure chance encounter, as all significant encounters are, especially those that lead to emotional involvement. But perhaps it is not a Tuesday. A Wednesday rather, or a Friday. Ah what's the difference which day of the week they meet. Who cares. But what a day, what a memorable day when Moinous & Sucette almost meet.

And is it raining. Pouring. That much is certain, otherwise the mood is all wrong. Yes, buckets full.

Sucette doesn't mind the rain. She has an umbrella. And for her rain always takes on sentimental connotations. Something to do perhaps with her temperament. Sucette is the sort of person who lets nature commiserate with her moods. Not that she comes from a rural background. Quite the contrary. A sophisticated Bostonian, she escapes into nature only in moments of crisis. As after her first abortion, to get over the psychological shock. Or during her second divorce. The first one happened too quickly to allow even a moment of pastoral reflection. And Sucette will probably seek nature again, out of confusion, when in the near future her paternal great-grandmother dies and leaves her the entire family inheritance.

Moinous hates it when it rains. Because of his hair and his pants. He never wears a hat, never. Except during his time in the army, when it was regulation. Those detestable G.I. caps and clumsy helmets that would mat down his hair. Nor does he carry an umbrella, never. So he's de-

pressed because the damn rain messes up his hair. His
dark brown hair which he combs straight back without a
part, quite long down the neck with a trace of a ducktail.
It's the style. And he is quite anal about the crease in his
pants. A leftover reflex from his days in the army. Two
years in the fucking paratroopers. Yes, drafted for a two-
year stretch. Still fresh in his mind since he's been out
only a few months. One of those miserable two years overseas, in the Far East. That certainly marks a young man
like Moinous, as Sucette will eventually discover. Indeed,
to the point of making her scream with frustration, later
when they have become intimate, and she watches him
button his shirts when he hangs them in her closet, carefully spacing the hangers with two fingers and facing each
one in the same direction. That's how deeply military life
got under his skin. In any case, his dislike of rain, his hair,
the crease in his pants, the leftover reflexes from the army,
these may seem like minor details, but revealing, revealing
indeed.

Moinous could carry an umbrella and thus avoid rainy
depressions. Umbrellas don't cost that much, even for
someone who is a bit short of cash, as is the case right
now. Nothing embarrassing about that. It's not a crime to
be broke. It's usually a temporary condition, rarely fatal.
In America especially, where all sorts of unexpected and
lucky opportunities can take a guy like Moinous right out
of his desperate financial difficulties. And who knows,
this may be his lucky day, in spite of the rain.

Yes, Moinous could carry an umbrella on rainy days,
even a used one, to avoid getting into a bad mood just because his hair and pants are wet. Lots of people carry um-

brellas in New York, during March, or February. And in most large European cities too. London, Paris, Hamburg, Copenhagen, Amsterdam. Ah yes, Amsterdam where it's wet all the time. Moinous is cosmopolitan enough to know that, in spite of his present situation. He may not have visited all these fascinating cities yet, but perhaps someday he will. With Sucette. Ah, that would be beautiful.

After all, Moinous was born in Europe. Yes, Paris, where he lived, or rather where he struggled with life until he was eighteen, and then emigrated to America, for reasons which he will eventually explain to Sucette when they become better acquainted, and she inquires about his past. Sucette is not the inquisitive type, but if she's going to get involved with a foreigner, at least she wants to know something of his background. But the fact that Moinous was born in France has to be mentioned now to avoid subsequent confusion and unnecessary retroactive explanations.

This means that Moinous speaks English with an accent. An abominable French accent, but which most native Americans who come in contact with him find charming and sexy, and that's in his favor in certain social situations.

The one time Moinous buys an umbrella, out of despair, or to gain a feeling of security, an expensive Knirps collapsible with a black silk cover and a leather handle, he forgets it at the movies on 42nd Street, where he often spends his afternoons on rainy days, and swears never to buy another one. It's a waste. And besides, once an umbrella is introduced in a love story, it sticks around till the end and quickly takes on awkward symbolic significations. And this because, according to Freud, the unconscious mental activity of an individual expresses itself consciously not only in obsessive thoughts but also in obsessive visual images. Later that would really complicate matters for Moinous & Sucette. So Moinous prefers to endure the rain without an umbrella, even if it puts him in a bad mood.

And he is certainly depressed the day he & Sucette smile at each other. And Sucette too, though not for the same reasons. Moinous because he is broke and jobless and on the verge of being evicted from his furnished room in the Bronx. Sucette because her life seems to be at a psychological impasse. They cannot possibly be aware of that, since they do not speak to each other that day. That doesn't mean, however, that they are not available for some sort of emotional encounter. At any rate, since Moinous is out of work it makes it possible for him to smile at Sucette on a weekday rather than on a weekend.

Unemployed, Moinous spends his days wandering aimlessly in the city. And to make matters worse, he is not eligible for unemployment compensation. A bureaucratic technicality, he's told repeatedly, which has to do with the types of jobs he's had since he's been discharged from the army. Plain bad luck. When it rains it pours for Moinous. So with nothing to do on a working day, he wanders around the city. He was fired from his last job, a couple of weeks ago. No problem then about having him walk all the way downtown to Washington Square, in spite of the rain.

He likes to walk on Washington Square. For sentimental reasons. He feeds the pigeons. Crumbs from the chunk of bread he usually brings with him on these solitary outings.

Talks to the pigeons. Looks at the arch, which reminds him nostalgically of another arch. The glorious Arc de Triomphe of his native Paris. The Washington arch is much smaller, of course, and much less imposing than the one on Place de l'Etoile. And the pigeons less exotic. But for Moinous, who has been living in self-imposed exile for almost five years, one of which, as noted, he spent in the Far East, any substitution, however unsatisfactory or unfulfilling it may be, of something he once loved, is a form of calmative.

Later, when they have become lovers, and Sucette is concerned about Moinous's fits of depression, or what he calls his *cafard*, she tells him that even though the soul of a displaced person is an empty region that cannot be approached or explored, nonetheless in America one always tries to overcome such weaknesses. This is not easy for Moinous. For as he is gradually and painfully discovering, America is a land where the impact of disillusion is spent in advance. A land of transparent duplication of old feelings and restless gestures. At least, that's what he feels while contemplating the Washington arch. Among the pigeons.

After all, l'Arc de Triomphe was built by the great Napoléon. Yes, on February 12, 1806. That's important for Moinous to know. It's even soothing at times for him to remember the bits of French history he learned before he was forced to drop out of school at the age of twelve, because of the war, the Second World War, and because of other unfortunate circumstances.

Sucette will often ask Moinous about this period of his life, especially when the two of them relapse into conversation after frantic moments of lovemaking. And he in turn will ask her about her childhood and adolescence in Boston. Love stories are always full of mutual reminiscences and personal revelations. That's what gives them intensity and depth.

What Moinous does not know, however, is that the Washington arch was erected in 1892, and that it is the last vestige of the dignity and taste of the wealthy settlers. Sucette knows this of course. It's part of her heritage. And she gives this information to Moinous one afternoon when they return to the place where they first smiled at each other. A sentimental pilgrimage they often make in the course of their love story.

In the five years since he's been in America, or as he specifies to Sucette the night they finally come together, Exactly four years, eleven months, and two days of misery and loneliness, Moinous has spent more time indulging in his private memories rather than trying to learn facts, useful facts, about the country where he now lives, and where he will probably continue to live for years to come. Unless, of course, he decides to commit suicide. A possibility he often contemplates in moments of rational despair. Or else decides to get out of this stinking country.

America, for Moinous, is a vast, perplexing conception. Loud and discordant. Crowded, frenetic, and elusive. Almost more than he can endure. In the past six months, since he was discharged from the army, he has often considered giving up on America. Not because he has failed here, but because America has failed him repeatedly. So he thinks. But to go where? Where? No, not back to France. There is nothing left for him there. Nothing that could possibly improve his life. If anything, it would make it worse.

As to suicide, Sucette explains to Moinous one evening when they are nearing the conditional disappointment of their relationship, though unaware of it then, but nonetheless terribly depressed, and Moinous proposes, with some measure of seriousness, a double suicide as a last resort, Sucette explains to Moinous, for she often ponders this question herself, that to commit the act of felo-de-se is a form of delusion. You see, my love, to leave one's life unfinished implies the possibility of success. What is left unlived may contain the potential truth one always seeks. Those who kill themselves do so with the conviction that they would have reached that truth eventually had they lived to the proper end. They die in the illusion of hope which in a way keeps the rest of us alive. Reason, therefore, for not committing suicide.

Moinous agrees. Indeed, Moinous rarely disagrees with Sucette. He finds her way of articulating abstract ideas so enchanting. Yes, he says, trying to remain on the same level of rhetoric as Sucette, suicide is always a false answer to an equally false question.

Well, I wouldn't put it quite that way. Because you see, darling, there are no false questions. All questions in life are true questions. Answers may be false, but questions cannot be false. Sure, they can be dumb, they can be stupid, but never false.

To this Moinous replies, I don't get it.

Look, Sucette continues, her lovely pale-blue eyes sparkling with intensity, for instance to ask if the moon is made of green cheese is not a false question. It's just a dumb question.

Oh, I see what you mean.

And at this point, thrilled, aroused even by their happy conclusion to the question of suicide, Moinous & Sucette reach out and embrace spontaneously. Clutching each other with abandon, they slowly recede into the alcove where the bed is located in Sucette's studio apartment. For a while the two of them loom frantically over an abyss of nudity before tumbling into ecstasy.

It will quite probably be Moinous's conviction in years to come, when Sucette is gone, though perhaps not forgotten, and he an old seedy optimist, that at least on this occasion, if never before or since, he achieved what he set out to do. After all, love or death is but the same thing in the end. In any event, may their passionate embrace be full of fury.

Suicide temporarily out of the question, and a return to his native country a futile consideration, Moinous, therefore, continues to indulge in his private memories. And that's understandable, for it takes years, many years of self-indulgence before a foreigner can break away from the past and overcome the nostalgic images of the place where he was born and raised, and where, supposedly, he reached the age of reason.

Moinous claims he reached the age of reason when he was fourteen years old. On a summer day in July, when he lost his virginity. Or thought he did. For even to this day he is not certain whether or not there was clear penetration or a mere premature ejaculation at the vaginal entrance of the farmer's wife who employed Moinous at the time. During the war.

At any rate, that's how he explains it to Sucette who is curious to learn how such a young and inexperienced Parisian found himself working on a farm in southern France during the war, and how he managed to make it, so precociously, with the farmer's wife.

Well, you see, Moinous elaborates, I was the only male on that farm during the occupation because all the men, I mean all the adult men, were off fighting the war somewhere in the underground, or else were locked up in some prison camp.

Moinous is the type of young man who wallows in the disorder of his obsessive imagination. For him the chaos of imagination always supersedes the order and veracity of facts. That is the basic condition of his existence. Except that Moinous makes no distinction, in his mind as well as in his life, between memory and imagination. That is perhaps why he has so little interest in facts. And Sucette often deplores this.

One late evening, as they are discussing a foreign film they have just seen at the Thalia about the life of a sculptor, and Moinous declares he often wishes he could become an artist or a poet, Sucette tells him, Well, who knows, you too may become famous one day. Perhaps a great painter or a renowned musician. Certainly not a writer though, because you have no ear for language, especially for the English language. A successful painter or musician, that's possible, but not before you're forty, and not before you start paying more attention to facts. The facts of life and the facts of history. Yes, someday you'll be a fantastic human being, when your intellect catches up with the uncontrolled experiences of your body, and when you realize that life is not made of vague emotions and imaginary situations, but of concrete facts rooted in historical events.

And Sucette will give Moinous lots of facts when the time comes, for she knows many facts, an incredible number. She's amazing about that. Yes, Sucette is a very factually oriented person. Has always been. When she was only six years old she could recite by heart the names of all forty-eight states and their capital cities. And she likes to share facts with others whenever possible. For Moinous his relation with Sucette will be like an education. A much needed intellectual and sentimental education.

For instance, one afternoon, over a cup of coffee, Sucette casually tells Moinous, Do you know that the Erie Canal was built in 1825, and that the first canal boat, the *Seneca Chief*, left Buffalo carrying two kegs of Lake Erie water which was later poured into the Atlantic Ocean in New York harbor? Lovers often have coffee together to exchange facts or recall pleasures. Moinous & Sucette are no exception. It is a way for them to calm their emotions during the intense moments of sensual pursuit. Cups of coffee punctuate the assaults on their bodies. And cigarettes too. All lovers live in the interstices of their lustful imagination.

Moinous & Sucette drink a lot of coffee together during their love story. And smoke many cigarettes. Gauloises.

Moinous always smokes French cigarettes, even after nearly five years in America. They cost a bit more than regular American cigarettes, and are not always available

in most drugstores. But they taste so much better, he tells
Sucette, who at first objects to the smell that lingers on his
clothes and on his breath. Moinous has to go out of his
way to buy his Gauloises, and that drives Sucette crazy in
the early weeks of their liaison.

However, soon after they reach intimacy, Sucette
switches from Pall Mall to Gauloises, even though at first
she finds them horrible. Too strong and too loosely
packed. Pieces of tobacco get stuck to the tongue, and she
dislikes the brownish stains they leave on her fingers. But
she quickly gets used to them and eventually enjoys
Gauloises even more than her ordinary American brand.

Moinous & Sucette like to give each other packs of cigarettes. Oh, by the way, darling, I got you some Gauloises
today while running some errands downtown, Sucette
says with a happy smile across her face. Me too, Moinous
remembers joyfully as he takes out several packs from his
coat pocket. It is a way for them to share in the little
thoughtful gestures of love.

It is not unusual for them to smoke a whole pack of
Gauloises during one of their blissful nights of lovemaking. But it is over cups of coffee that they share the most.
In fact, had they spoken to each other on Washington
Square, rather than simply smile, they would probably
have gone for coffee together in order to get acquainted.
And also to get out of the rain. Perhaps to Schrafft's, on
Fifth Avenue. Sucette's favorite coffee shop. Or else they
would have gone to Sucette's apartment, on 105th Street,
between Riverside Drive and West End Avenue. That does
not mean they would have made love immediately, even
though the desire may have been there. It's just that Su-

cette likes the comfort of her apartment, and loves to have people over.

And that's most likely where they will go, Schrafft's, to have coffee, when they eventually meet again, since it is destined to happen. Let's say two or three weeks after the exchange of smiles on Washington Square. Once again accidentally. But uptown this time. Perhaps in Rockefeller Center. Oh yes, at the Librairie Française, where Moinous happens to be looking at a mystery novel of the Série Noire, and Sucette is inquiring about the latest novel by Simone de Beauvoir. *Les Mandarins.* She knows French quite well. Learned it as a young girl in a boarding school in Switzerland. Somewhat of a requirement in my kind of background, she later explains to Moinous, who wants to know where she learned French so well. The happiest years of my childhood, she adds softly as her eyes darken.

You know something, Moinous remarks, it's really unusual for an American to know French that well. I mean it's such a tough language. I only wish I could speak English that good.

Yes, that's where they will probably meet and speak. At the Librairie Française. Two or three weeks later, when they bump into each other again. And this time, for sure, they'll go for coffee. Their first quiet cups of coffee together in a long series of such interludes until the final disappointment.

Would you like a cup of coffee? is the first thing Sucette always asks when Moinous comes to visit in her apartment, after they meet again and eventually fall in love. In Sucette's case, however, these invitations to coffee are a way of delaying corporeal confrontation. Not that she is prudish, or that sex frightens her. It's just that it takes time for her to let go. Sensitive and somewhat shy, even though older and certainly more worldly than Moinous, Sucette moves from seemingly timid babble to helpless silence whenever she is alone with a man. And so, it is over cups of coffee that she presents Moinous with facts. Some simple and useful. Others so complex and so elaborate that Moinous does not usually grasp their immediate usefulness.

In any event, Moinous doesn't know that the Erie Canal was built in 1825, and isn't sure what to do with this information. But he pretends to be interested, and while sipping his coffee asks Sucette, How did you find out all this stuff? And where is the Erie Canal? I've never even heard of it.

That's what I mean, Sucette says. You're only interested in yourself. You never want to learn anything about the world. But maybe that's why I love you so much. There is something so innocent, so careless about you. She reaches out to Moinous and touches his face. Then she tells him that the Erie Canal starts in Buffalo and goes all the way to Albany where it then joins with the Hudson River down to the Atlantic, and this way, you see, it forms a direct waterway from the Great Lakes to the ocean. Here, let me show you, Sucette says as she takes down an atlas of the United States from her bookshelves and opens it to the map of New York State. She stands next to Moinous, who is still seated, and points to the canal on the map, following its course with her finger from Buffalo to the Atlantic.

From his armchair Moinous reaches around Sucette's waist and holds her left breast. Without reacting to the pressure of his hand, Sucette goes on explaining that she herself found out about the Erie Canal while visiting friends in Buffalo. A very interesting young couple who used to live here in New York. You would like them. He's a psychologist, and she's a schoolteacher. Marvelous people. Sucette hesitates as Moinous's hand moves down her hip. Then she adds, her voice rising to a higher pitch, Very dedicated people, and extremely knowledgeable. They were sent upstate to work in the steel mills in order to. She stops in the middle of her sentence as if something prevents her from going on. Please, stop that, not now, she says, gently pushing Moinous's hand away. She steps aside to replace the atlas on the shelf. How about another cup of coffee? she asks in her normal tone of voice. It's still hot.

Moinous finds the information about the Erie Canal fascinating, but he wonders why Sucette stopped talking so abruptly about her friends in Buffalo. He is about to ask why they were sent there to work in the steel mills, and by whom, but Sucette is now serving the fresh cups of coffee, and he forgets to ask.

Is the coffee hot enough? Sucette inquires as she sits across from Moinous in her armchair and lights a cigarette.

Yes, delicious, Moinous replies, as he too lights a cigarette. The two of them sit in silence for a while. Love stories are always full of such moments.

Sucette seems preoccupied. She keeps replacing a loose strand of hair behind her ear. Moinous's mind is drifting. He is trying to visualize mentally the two kegs of Lake Erie water on the deck of the *Seneca Chief*. A smile appears at the corner of his mouth. It's so nice to sit here with you, he says to Sucette. I learn so much from you about this great country.

Sucette does not answer. She simply reaches out and squeezes Moinous's hand. A little redness appears on her generous face. Yes, it's so good, so good to have someone to talk to sometimes. You don't know how important it is.

Moinous tries hard to remember all these facts about America, for future reference. But the trouble with him, as Sucette will soon discover, is that he cannot always remember what is complicated, and he often forgets what is simple.

Nevertheless, Sucette has such a charming way of sharing facts with others that she never makes the other person feel ignorant or inferior. On the contrary, she uses her knowledge to enhance her relation with others and make them feel at ease. Her propensity for facts keeps the conversation going. However, she never presents them in the form of a probing question, but always as a casual declaration, so that the knowledge seems to be already there in the other, and has simply been forgotten or misplaced. Moinous really appreciates this. But besides knowing facts, Sucette also carries the burden of her past. Her unhappy childhood and disastrous adolescence in New England. Perhaps not as miserable, and certainly not as confused as Moinous's, but difficult nonetheless. Sucette too has had her painful moments of disappointment and disillusionment. Especially with her family. Ah yes, her good old New England family.

Moinous will eventually meet all the members of Sucette's family. That's inevitable. On a weekend trip to Boston, several months after the accidental encounter and the exchange of smiles on Washington Square. Of course, in order for that to happen the two potential lovers will have to meet again, speak to each other, and subsequently become intimate.

Perhaps, the second time, they will meet in the subway. Or in one of the big department stores on Fifth Avenue where Moinous likes to wander when he has nothing else to do, even though he can never afford to buy anything. Except once, on impulse. On a rainy day. An umbrella, at Saks Fifth Avenue, on the ground floor. A black one with a leather handle. Yes, the very same umbrella he leaves behind at the movies on 42nd Street.

Or else they will meet in the streets, in some other part of the city. Uptown. By chance.

Why not the Librairie Française. Yes, where Moinous often stops to look at the French books when he's in the neighborhood. Though again he cannot afford to buy these expensive books. And Moinous is so happy because since that rainy afternoon on Washington Square, he's been thinking a lot about the charming blonde who smiled at him so compassionately. And Sucette too is delighted.

They will recognize each other. Hesitantly at first. And then once more exchange mutual smiles. But this time they speak to each other. Go for coffee to become better acquainted. At Schrafft's, Sucette suggests. And soon after, well not immediately, but eventually, they become lovers. That's how it usually happens.

A few months later Sucette proposes a trip to Boston for

the weekend to visit her family. It's her great-grandmother's ninety-fifth birthday. What an extraordinary
weekend it will be.

At first Moinous doesn't understand why Sucette wants
him to meet her family. Why she insists on this trip up to
Boston. By train. There is no talk of marriage, or anything
like that, between them, even though they are now living
together in Sucette's apartment, on 105th Street. Certainly
not. That would be so incongruous, in spite of the ruses of
desire. They are so ill-matched. And there is the difference
in age between them. Almost ten years. But Moinous goes
and meets The Clique, as Sucette calls her family.

Sucette's father. A tall, angular man with thin lips, a
strong chin, sleek white hair that clings close to his high-
vaulted skull. Chairman of the board of some corporation
or other, Sucette explains later on. A standoffish man, not
very affable, who speaks only in monosyllables. What did
you say your last name is, young man? he asks Moinous after a brusque handshake upon their first man-to-man
meeting in the library of the huge old house where Sucette
was raised. It is not easy for Moinous to react correctly
with such a person. Being there, being present in front of
this man, in front of what appears to be a monument of
righteousness, he feels compromised and doesn't know if
he should drop to the floor and crawl in silence, or if he
should leap on the antique desk in the library and become
a brawling superman of arrogance.

Sucette's mother. Still quite attractive for her age. Late
fifties. Very blond and charming, but stern and waspish to
the tips of her fingernails. Extremely inquisitive. She
keeps asking Moinous about his life, his work, his parents,

his plans, his ambitions. Moinous tries to avoid her squinting eyes as he mumbles vague answers. To his surprise, he notices how terribly flat-chested she is, even though Sucette is rather buxom. And her sister too. Yes, that weekend Moinous also meets Sucette's sister, who lives with husband and children in the family house.

Two years younger than Sucette, the sister is stunningly beautiful. Savagely seductive with her sandy-blond hair. But fidgety and insecure. Everyone in the family keeps mentioning her nervousness and insecurity, and that makes her even more nervous and insecure. She seems quite taken with Moinous, who senses that something interesting could unfold between them if they were left to themselves. Moinous, who has remained very French in his attitude toward women finds *les femmes américaines* to be too self-explanatory. The trouble, however, is that the explanation keeps changing. And what makes it even more troublesome, in the case of the sister, is that the provocation of her body is tempered by the elegance of her clothes and the savoir-faire of her gestures. This confuses him, as everything else does in America.

Indeed, Moinous often wonders about his failure to adapt to a world which is so out of step with its ideals. Often wonders, in spite of his pernicious and incurable optimism, why he abandoned the rationality of Europe, however unreal and obsolete it may be, for the temptation of trying to achieve comfort, and perhaps even success, in such a disjointed reality.

Moinous tells Sucette, when they are alone for a moment during the weekend, that her sister is making big eyes at him. And Sucette retorts, Oh I'm not surprised, my sister is always ready to jump into bed with the first guy who smiles at her. Go ahead, if that's what you want. I don't care.

No no, that's not what I mean. I was just. And Moinous blushes.

And besides, Sucette tells him, one does not say Making big eyes in English. It's not correct. One says Making eyes. Sucette often corrects the little mistakes Moinous makes in his adopted tongue, even though he argues in his defense that the English language is totally irrational.

Okay, Moinous tries to explain, but in France we say Faire les gros yeux when somebody makes a pass at you.

Well, maybe in France, but now you're in America. You better get used to that. Sucette does not always correct Moinous with such a sarcastic tone of voice, but this time she is irritated. The whole weekend is turning into a disaster. Especially with the sister's husband.

A self-impressed braggard with no feeling for others, Sucette's brother-in-law is a big loud bully of a man in search of a destination, but who pretends to have reached it. The only son of one of the best families in Boston, Sucette whispers to Moinous when she sees his puzzled look upon being introduced to the brother-in-law. He knocked up my sister when she was in college, Bennington, and they had to get married. They've been living here in this house ever since. Almost ten years now. He used to play football. For Army or Navy, I forget which.

The brother-in-law, freckled and puffy, constantly teases people, including his own three lovely daughters. But especially his wife, whom he treats with unabashed vulgarity. How do you like my gorgeous wife? he asks Moinous as he pats her on the rump. Wouldn't you want to play with that if you had a chance? Hey man, look at those boobs.

Matthew, please, stop that, you're embarrassing me, the sister whines as she pushes him away, tossing her head aside so that her blond mane flies sensuously across her face. Moinous is horrified by this scene, and consequently fails to recognize the voluptuous look Sucette's sister throws his way from behind the screen of her hair.

Somehow, the brother-in-law and Moinous manage to become buddies during the weekend because of their army experiences, even though there is a difference in age, and evidently they were not of the same rank. Moinous made only corporal, in the paratroopers, and even then he got busted to Pfc because of a dumb mistake in Tokyo. The brother-in-law was a captain in the Marines, he explains. No, he does not explain, he asserts in a commanding voice while laughing at his own embarrassing Marine Corps stories.

Nonetheless, he is impressed that Moinous was with the tough 82nd Airborne Division, and that he made forty-seven jumps out of a plane. Three in combat, Moinous specifies. In Korea. Not the most ideal type of terrain for parachuting with all those crummy rice paddies. I tell you, I'm lucky I didn't get hurt, or even killed over there. The brother-in-law never went overseas. He trained the dumb recruits somewhere in Texas, he giggles. But now he's in the reserves.

Much of the conversation, when the whole family is gathered, especially during the sumptuous meals served by the two maids, Margie and Molly, centers around Matthew's and Moinous's adventures in the service. Matthew during the Second World War, Moinous in the Korean War. These army reminiscences make it somewhat easier for Moinous to endure the weekend. It also gives him a chance to boast about how he served America even though he was not yet a citizen. But now I am an American, he declares emphatically. I became a citizen in Tokyo, a year ago.

Oh my goodness, how could that happen? Sucette's mother inquires with a supercilious smile which Moinous interprets as a sign of curiosity and a signal for him to tell the story of how he became a citizen in such unusual circumstances. The whole family is sitting around the dinner table, the first evening of Moinous & Sucette's visit to Boston.

You see, Moinous begins after clearing his throat and half rising from his chair to better tell his story, During the Korean War a new law was passed by the Congress of the United States. Before that you had to wait five years, and you could become a citizen only on American soil. But this new law made it possible for people who were overseas to become citizens on foreign land, and after only a few months in the service. I think three months, or something like that. So they gathered all the foreigners, I mean all the foreign soldiers who were serving in the U.S. Army in the Far East, and brought them to Tokyo. I was in a foxhole then, near Inchon, and let me tell you, it was rough. I mean cold as hell. And those little guys kept coming at us from all sides. Anyway, the captain of my outfit called me and said, Corporal, get your gear together and your ass moving, eh, you're on your way to Tokyo. That's exactly what he said to me. I was a corporal at the time in charge of a sixty-millimeter-mortar squad. What's going on? I asked. Don't know, the captain answered. The order just came in for you to report immediately to General Headquarters in Tokyo. Not the foggiest idea what it's all about, but dammit must be important, just when I need every goddamn man I've got.

You see, Moinous explains, we were getting ready for this new offensive. A big spring offensive. It was in March. Or perhaps April. Moinous takes a sip of wine from the finely etched half-filled crystal goblet in front of him, and continues.

What the hell do they want with me? I said to myself. But of course, I didn't argue. An order is an order when you're in the army. Right. Moinous pauses as he looks at the brother-in-law, who gives him an approving nod. And besides, Moinous goes on, I was so glad to get out of that mud pile. So I packed my stuff in my duffel bag and got on this Air Force plane which flew me to Tokyo. I was excited about going to Tokyo, as you can well imagine. You know, the nightlife and all that. Especially after more than six months in a foxhole on the front line. Wow was I horny. And nervous too because I had no idea what this was all about. In Tokyo they gathered all of us foreigners. Hungarians, Poles, Italians, Rumanians, you know, all kinds of foreigners, even two Arabs. I was the only Frenchman in the group. Then they explained to us that we were going to be naturalized. They even issued new uniforms for everybody, and we had a full dress rehearsal before the big day.

Moinous is getting so excited by his story that he is now

standing up and gesticulating like a puppet. When the day came, he goes on, we all assembled in this huge auditorium at the Ernie Pyle Center. It's like a recreation center in Tokyo where they have billiards, bowling alleys, Ping-Pong tables, movies, and all sorts of things like that for the soldiers to relax. It's really a great place. You can even meet girls there, nice American girls, I mean, when they have dances. Anyway, we were sitting in the auditorium, very sharp and spit-shined in our new uniforms, and they had all these officers in full parade dress, and even two generals for the occasion. One of them a three-star general, because you see it was an important historic event. First time, you understand, first time in the history of this country that foreigners were being naturalized overseas. The generals made speeches about America, about freedom, and duty, and responsibility, you know, junk like that. Then an orchestra played music. A military band. They played all these bombastic tunes like *The Star Spangled Banner. America the Beautiful. God Bless America.* It was very nice. After the music our names were called alphabetically. The colonel who called the names had difficulties pronouncing some of them. When he came to my name he got it all wrong and everybody laughed, including the two generals. And I did too.

Moinous stops a moment to smile and clear his throat while the whole family waits for the rest of the story, forks and knives neatly resting on the plates. When my turn came I went up on the stage, from the right side. Shook hands with the officers who formed a line up there, and with the two generals in the middle who congratulated me. It was not easy, you see, because first you had to salute and then shake hands, with the same hand, while grabbing your diploma with the other hand. But we had rehearsed, so nobody really goofed too much. After that you walked across the stage, saluting and shaking hands with all the other officers. At the end of the line there was a guy who took your picture. I still have it. Someday, Sucette, remind me to show it to you. I really look great in my paratrooper uniform. On the left side of the stage there was a sergeant. I still remember his face well. All red and puffy. A big fat sonofa, oops, excuse me, who gave each of us a little American flag. There was a box full of them because there must have been more than a hundred of us foreigners becoming citizens that day. You know, those little flags you put on cakes.

Moinous stops talking and draws in the air, in front of his face, with his index finger, a little imaginary rectangle. Then we went back to our seats holding the diploma in one hand and the flag in the other. It felt stupid.

When I was back in my seat, I looked at this little flag, and you won't believe what was written on the side. Like this, up and down, on the side: MADE IN JAPAN. No I'm not kidding. That's what it said. MADE IN JAPAN. I mean, the flag, the flag was made in Japan. Can you believe that?

Moinous stops and sits down, expecting a reaction to his story. As he pulls his chair closer to the table he knocks his fork to the floor. His head under the table, he waits for the reaction. Perhaps even some laughter. A touch of polite laughter. After all it is a funny story. But no one around the table says anything. Except finally, Sucette's father, after a long silence and a little cough. Well, I guess that was the best way for them to take care of this matter since it is the law. It would have been too much trouble for them to bring all these people back to the States. Or to ship American-made flags to Japan.

As he emerges from under the table holding his fork, Moinous looks at Sucette imploringly, sort of asking if he goofed in telling this story. She gives him an almost imperceptible reassuring nod, which he interprets as meaning, It's okay, it's okay. But he knows, he knows, it's not okay.

The conversation drifts to something else. The brother-in-law is now telling one of his Marine Corps stories. Half-listening while chewing a piece of meat, a rather·delicious piece of roast beef au jus, Moinous reflects on how remarkable it is that such an ordinary consciousness as the brother-in-law somehow always manages to entertain a human dialogue even in the midst of the most uncongenial situation. If only Moinous could be like that. But unfortunately for him, when talking with people like these he has a feeling that he must constantly account for the embarrassing circumstances of his being. He may have escaped the big-scale xenophobic pomposity of Europe, but now he must confront and endure the Disneyland mentality of America.

Fuck them, Moinous thinks, now chewing the baked potatoes. I yam what I yam and that's all that I yam, he says to himself in piteous self-justification. Not aware, of course, that he has mentally echoed Popeye the sailorman. But that's how this toot toot American gets under your skin and into your bones if you don't watch out. In this land of comic-book mentality, the self will dash its hopes without any help from the outside if given time to prey on itself. Moinous is no exception. He is quickly learning that the attainment of hope and success in America creates an equal aching void to take the place of unfulfilled hope and desire. It will take Moinous a long time, and many more disastrous encounters with people such as these, to realize that hope never ceases to be a torture.

Later, he will tell Sucette. You know something, I don't think I'll ever understand your family.

And Sucette will tell him. Maybe that's because here in America people are not what they say they are, whereas in Europe they are what they say they are.

Well, I don't know. I'm not sure you've got it right, Moinous answers. I think it's the reverse. Sometimes I have the feeling it's easier to know the people you're talking to when they lie about themselves rather than when they tell the truth. But that's not the case with your family. They confuse me with their looks of integrity. They make me feel insignificant and poor.

That's exactly what I mean, Sucette replies. My family is inscrutable. The order and sanctity of their Puritanism screen the ontological weaknesses of their lives. You see, they always identify poverty less with evil than with unimportance. That's why they are so unintelligible to an outsider like you. Or at least, think they are. And why you are so insignificant to them.

Then why the hell did you bring me here? Moinous cries out. To humiliate me?

No, darling, not to humiliate you, but to confirm our love, Sucette answers as her face softens with tenderness.

Suddenly Moinous realizes that from being a lover in Sucette's comfortable New York apartment, here, in this stuffy Boston house he has become a mere situation. He is about to burst into rage when he notices how Sucette's mouth is now set in a bitter grimace and her eyes full of pain like those of a martyr whose body bristles with arrows. Moinous reaches for Sucette's hand and squeezes it. Oh but I do love you, I do, I swear, in spite of them. However, for the first time in his life Moinous understands what quicksand love is.

Nevertheless, Moinous has never met people like these. How could he have? Not in the kind of sordid life he's led up to now in America. First two years working in a Detroit factory, then the next two years in the army, as a draftee, and now jobless in New York. Consequently, with the little experience he has, he cannot recognize how typical, how stereotypical these people are. And that's even true of the three lovely blond daughters of Sucette's sister.

Nine, seven, and six. Immaculately scrubbed and groomed, always dressed in matching jumpsuits or sailor dresses, they too act as if they have been programmed by some ultramoral superpolite mechanism. However, the presence of Moinous in the house seems to have disrupted their behavior. During the entire weekend they look at him with flirty adoring blue eyes. And since Moinous loves little girls, always has, and even knows by instinct how to deal with them on their own level, he keeps smiling at Sucette's nieces or making funny faces at them whenever he has a chance and no one is looking. The three little dolls cannot refrain from giggling and from wiggling their charming derrières as they chase up and down the stairs to hide in the secret nooks and crannies of this enormous house, even though their grandmother constantly reprimands and reminds them to behave.

That weekend, Moinous also meets Sucette's great-grandmother on her father's side, whose ninety-fifth birthday is being celebrated. All my other grandparents are dead, Sucette explains, but this one is like Plymouth Rock. She believes she's historically immortal, and so far seems to have proved it. Totally senile, but remarkably sprightly, she scoots around the house in an electric wheelchair, bumping into the furniture, knocking over the plants as she mumbles under her breath. At the dining table she presides at one end, but usually falls asleep by the second course. Sucette is very fond of her great-grandmother, even though the old lady does not recognize her and keeps asking who that is whenever Sucette enters the room.

Yes, Moinous meets all of them in Boston, during that extraordinary weekend. Including Thomas, the butler, who's been with the family for over thirty-five years, and the two maids, Margie and Molly, both rather plump and imperious, but friendly with Moinous, within the limits of their domestic capacity. Perhaps they sense that he would be more comfortable talking, or even flirting with them in the kitchen, than making conversation with the family at the dining table.

Moinous feels miserably out of place in this environment. Perhaps that is Sucette's intent. She wants him to know where she comes from. What her background is. And so on. Just in case. But it's not easy for Moinous to understand this milieu, and to fit in. And it gets more and more unbearable as the weekend progresses. It's one of those long three-day weekends.

By the second evening at dinner, Moinous is totally ignored. No one is talking to him anymore. The conversation is all about the family. How Sucette's poor aunt Beth still hasn't recovered from her husband's sudden death, you remember Uncle George of course, who had that fatal seizure last spring, what a pity, such a fine, gentle man, and how Aunt Beth is still perturbed that Sucette could not make it to the funeral, it's really a shame, and how the whole family, yes Aunt Beth too, is planning to spend the month of July in the New Hampshire cottage, and will Sucette be able to join them, it would be so wonderful to have everybody together for once, and how Father has been working so hard lately, you know, with the way the economy is going, those goddamn commies are ruining the country, and how Matthew is seriously considering running for office in the next election, as Lieutenant-Governor of Massachusetts, yes he's been approached, and how Mother is seeing a specialist for her anxieties, oh nothing really serious, and how the three darling girls are doing so well in school, and how Sucette's sister is hoping to get away to Europe with a friend in a couple of months, it will be so much fun and so relaxing, if only Sucette could come along, but she's so busy in New York, on and on and on.

Blahblahblah, blahblahblah, Moinous grumbles to himself as he is getting more and more annoyed. And embarrassed too, because the men have to wear jackets for dinner, and the sleeves of his sport coat are worn through at the elbows and he tries to keep them tucked below the table while eating, which is not very comfortable, and on top of that he doesn't know which of the three forks he's supposed to use for the fish, and Sucette is hardly paying attention to him now, and he feels like getting up from the table to go and hide in the bathroom for a while, and perhaps even cry.

As Moinous sits there, crushed by his own superfluous presence and the lurking insecurities of his being, he has a sudden urge to scream, to jump up and down and scream in the middle of all that politely hushed clank of the serving dishes and that sweet buzzing of conversation. He feels like shouting vile obscenities. Something like, Fuck you all and your fucking lovely family life. Perhaps even in French. *Allez tous vous faire enculer dans les miches.* Moinous often regresses into the safety of his native tongue whenever he is troubled. Of course, that would not be very civilized. But then Moinous could explain, paraphrasing Freud, that the first man who hurled a foul word at his adversary was the true founder of civilization.

Instead, as the voice of the brother-in-law gets louder and louder since he's now explaining his political views, and his gestures more and more uncontrolled, and he loses all human attributes as he turns into a wild beast, his voice becoming a groan and his hands gigantic paws, Moinous begins to undress the people around the table. Except Sucette, who seems to have fallen asleep in the middle of the brother-in-law's vociferations, her head resting on her folded arms on the table.

Moinous sees Sucette's mother sitting upright across from him with bare breasts bursting out of her blouse which she has unbuttoned with quick nervous fingers. She is holding her breasts with her hands and thrusting them at Moinous. They are small and wrinkled, but with large brown nipples that stare at Moinous like tired eyes. Without abandoning her supercilious expression, she strokes her breasts and leans over the table to offer them, and the thick milk now dripping from the swollen nipples, to the guest of honor, as her mouth splits open and Moinous notices, for the first time, the huge gap between her two front teeth.

Sucette's father, meanwhile, is standing naked at the head of the table. His skin is pale, pale bluish like that of a corpse, and hairless. He has an enormous erection protruding out of his foreskin above his deflated cullions, and the old penis is all red, crimson red, and he too leans forward, his skinny thighs pressed hard against the edge of the table, and he places his raw burning member in his stemmed crystal glass and shakes it with two fingers as the iced water splashes over, and his thin lips break into a painful grimace.

Sucette's sister is on her knees, her dress pulled up to her furry golden crotch, and she is fondling Moinous's fly while panting and drooling from the mouth, and with trembling but expert fingers she extricates his phallus which brusquely swells in her hand, and she slides it in her mouth and sucks it with wet abandon.

On the other side of the table, Sucette's three lovely nieces have taken off their sailor dresses and discarded their lace panties. They are giggling and rolling on the carpeted floor while fingering each other's rosy twats. And even the great-grandmother is involved. She has removed her false teeth from her mouth and is playing with them on the table, making the complete set of yellowish dentures, upper and lower, walk and talk like some miniature monster among the silver, the crystal and the porcelain, knocking over the glasses, as she goes quack-quack, click-click, with her empty mouth all sucked in.

While all this is going on, Margie and Molly, quite unconcerned, continue to circulate around the table, picking up the glasses, refilling them with wine, removing dishes. The whole scene unwinds like the reel of a silent movie, except for the quackquacks and clickclicks of the great-grandmother.

Slouched in his chair, legs wide apart, Moinous is ready to explode and abuse the inside of the sister's mouth when, all of a sudden, the brother-in-law, who all the while has been going on with his political ranting, knocks over his glass of wine with a sweeping gesture. The red liquid slowly spreads on the white damask tablecloth. The blood-like stain brings everyone back to the formality of the moment, and at once they are all properly seated and dressed. Sucette is awake, rubbing her eyes with the back of her hand. The others are staring at the clumsy brother-in-law with sanctimonious eyes. Then the conversation buzzes again in its normal flow. Margie and Molly have rushed to wipe the spilt wine and refill the glasses.

Moinous murmurs an excuse, to no one in particular, gets up, and goes to the bathroom. He locks the door. Drops his pants to his feet, and with angry frustration masturbates violently in front of the mirror until he ejaculates in the sink. He turns the water on and watches his sperm go down the drain.

Later, at the end of the weekend, on the express train back to New York City, Moinous tells Sucette about his fantastic vision of her family at the dinner table.

Don't you think, Sucette asks, not even trying to hide her irritation, that such puerile fantasies show a twisted imagination and a lack of emotional unity?

We all live like cockroaches in the crevices of our twisted imagination, Moinous retorts. We fluctuate between glandular activity and pure sensuality, between loneliness and mental discomfort. Somewhere in there our emotions float like wrecks, and there never is any emotional unity. Besides, such unity is impossible since we don't know whether emotions are based in the body or if they originate in the mind. So don't give me all that stuff about twisted imagination and lack of emotional unity.

What's gotten into you? Sucette's face is all flushed now as she continues the argument. That's not what I was asking. Who is talking about the split between mind and body. You always misunderstand everything I say. I was merely expressing an opinion about fantasy. And anyway, I warned you about my family.

Well, keep your opinions to yourself, Moinous replies, obviously disturbed. And next time don't ask me to go with you to Boston. Their first fight. First inevitable lovers' quarrel. And for the rest of the train ride back to New York they hardly talk to each other. Sucette seemingly engrossed in the novel she is reading. Lie Down in Darkness, by William Styron. Moinous staring out of the train window at the rainy New England landscape. Yes, it is raining again.

Of course, all this happens several months after the exchange of smiles on Washington Square. Smiles which will lead to nothing unless Moinous & Sucette meet again, by chance.

Between this second chance encounter, at the Librairie

Française, and the disastrous weekend in Boston, Moinous will become better acquainted with Sucette. He will learn all about her life and background during their intimate conversations. Except that it will be a slow, gradual revelation. For unlike Moinous, who gladly squanders his inner life without any restraint, Sucette does not reveal herself easily. She is prudent with spoken words. She has been forced into prudence of language and manners early in her youth, and only as she grows older does she learn romance and the gestures of passion. The natural sequel of an unnatural beginning. Consequently, Sucette operates out of the grating dissimilarity of extremes, in the imaginary void where they merge. So it takes time for her to reveal to Moinous the details of her two abortions, her one miscarriage, her nervous breakdown, and her two divorces. All this and more she gradually tells Moinous in the long hours they spend together talking. Talking and loving each other, of course. During the long hours of night especially. Sitting close to each other, or lying in bed, bodies entwined. Most love stories are nocturnal. That's what makes them fascinating.

But as she stands on Washington Square, that rainy afternoon, time must seem endless to Sucette in the prospect of her future involvement with Moinous. And vice versa. Since they are both in a state of emotional availability within the confines of their loneliness, anything can happen. Except that neither of them can anticipate the consequences of their love story. That's always the case. The quick smiles they exchange may be enough to engender that story, but not enough to reveal the intensity of its hope, nor the fury of its conditional disappointment.

That day, however, unlike Moinous, who has nothing better to do but wander aimlessly in the city, Sucette has a reason for being on Washington Square. A political reason. Besides, she doesn't have a steady job. Doesn't need one. She has private means. That's why she can be in the Village on a regular workday. She too is unemployed, in a manner of speaking, but not because she was fired, or laid off, or anything like that. No, Sucette has never really had to work. Except during the period when she ran away from home, at the age of twenty-seven, and no one knew where she had gone. For two years she worked in a factory in Brooklyn. Completely cut off from family support, she had to work, or she would have starved. Though at the time there was another reason, an idealistic reason, for her to take this factory job. When she arrived in New York from Boston, Sucette joined a Communist cell as a gesture of rebellion against her family and her background, and it is as a Fellow Traveler that she was assigned a job in a Brooklyn factory to try and indoctrinate her fellow workers.

This was five years ago. Almost five years. At about the same time Moinous arrived in America from France. And now Moinous is starving. Well, almost. But that's nothing new for him. Most of his life he's been suffering the humiliation of poverty and deprivation. This is why Sucette's smile on Washington Square means so much to him, even though she does not speak to him on that occasion. That smile represents a touch of human contact, full of compassion, inadvertent as it may be, in the bleak solitude of his present situation. Moinous is not very good at reading signs, especially Anglo-Saxon signs. Or rather, he often misreads the signs others send him. He quickly gets carried away. For no sooner does Moinous put his body in order than his mind trips him.

Even though Sucette has now drifted away from her involvement with her Fellow Travelers, it is for political reasons that she is on Washington Square that day, in spite of the rain. She came by taxi from her cozy apartment on 105th Street. She has a purpose that afternoon. Yes, a political purpose. She is participating in an anti-McCarthy demonstration. This is the period when The Senator from Wisconsin is doing his red-baiting. Like millions of other outraged Americans who have finally caught on to his demagogical tactics, Sucette is very disturbed by The Senator's reckless accusations, and on that day has decided to do something about it. Whereas Moinous has no specific purpose for being here, except perhaps to look at the arch, or talk to the pigeons. In English or in French, depending on his mood, or in both simultaneously. Especially to the one-legged pigeon with whom Moinous has established a friendly relationship.

Moinous notices that crippled bird one day when he sits dejectedly on a bench in the Square, pitying himself because he's just lost his job. This seems to happen to him with some regularity. He takes out his sandwich from his coat pocket, unwraps it, and slowly chews on the two dry slices of white bread with a piece of domestic Swiss cheese in between. The bird hops over on one leg. At first Moinous thinks the other leg is folded under into the bird's feathery belly. Nothing unusual about that. Moinous has seen pictures of birds standing on one leg. Pink flamingos. Storks. But on closer inspection, and particularly since the bird keeps tumbling over onto its side like a drunkard, Moinous realizes that indeed this bird has only one leg. What are you, my poor little fellow, some kind of handicapped war veteran? Moinous asks, attempting a smile of compassion in the midst of his self-pitying mood. He throws a piece of bread on the ground. The pigeon pecks at it while balancing himself precariously on one leg, then looks up and gives a little squeak. An almost human squeak which nearly brings tears to Moinous's eyes. From that day on, Moinous and the one-legged pigeon become fast friends. They see each other regularly by the same bench, whenever Moinous comes down to Washington Square.

However, the day Moinous & Sucette smile at each other, the pigeons are not there on the Square. Not because of the rain. Pigeons are well-known for being rainproof. But because of the demonstration. Or rather they are not hopping on the ground carefree as usual, but gloomily perched high up on the arch, away from the crowd. Therefore, Moinous cannot talk to his one-legged friend, even though he thinks he sees him, way at the top of the arch, dripping with rain. Moinous doesn't know about the demonstration. He just stumbles into it, and indeed is very surprised to see so many people assembled on the Square in such bad weather. Maybe two hundred or three hundred of them, he estimates as he mingles with the demonstrators.

Moinous likes to walk in the streets of New York when he has nothing else to do. Alone. For hours. Even five years after first seeing this city, he is still astonished by the beauty, by the grandiose magnificence of this amazing city. Its incredible shape, and the way the streets and the avenues crisscross in neat patterns to form blocks, as they are called here. The spectacular buildings. Those immense towers that reach into the sky. Those skyscrapers. And the wind, ah the relentless wind that blows through these corridors of glass walls and brings tears to your eyes, especially late at night when you're walking all alone. This is how Moinous described New York City in a letter to a friend back in France, soon after he arrived in America, trying to be as poetic as he could to give his friend a real sense of how fantastic this city is, though the friend never answered. Unless the reply got lost in the mail, Moinous speculated. For at the time he still thought, as most foreigners do, that letters from Europe often get lost in the mail. In any event, this was the end of his correspondence with his friend in France. Nevertheless, five years later, Moinous still finds New York fascinating.

And especially the people. Ah the mass of people in the streets. All of them rushing from one part of the city to another with such intensity, and always carrying packages or boxes or briefcases or suitcases. Moinous never carries anything like that. Except, of course, when he stops at the grocery store on his way home to his furnished room in the Bronx to buy a loaf of bread or some cheese or a box of noodles or other essentials like these for survival. So many interesting people one can meet in New York, by chance. If only Moinous knew how to take advantage of chance encounters, he could talk to some of these people as he wanders in the streets, and these fortuitous encounters could lead to unusual situations. Perhaps even result in love affairs.

Yes, Moinous likes to walk in the city in search of the unexpected. Walking alone gives him a chance to contemplate his problems and sort out his confused inner life. Not without a touch of self-pity. But that's justifiable. Two weeks already without a job, and at most three dollars left to survive, and nothing in sight. Nothing. No need to whine about it, Moinous says to himself. These are hard times. Lots of other guys in the same lousy situation.

Sucette doesn't have to worry about such problems of daily survival. She has her income. But she cares about humanity, and about injustice and civil rights. She does indeed. That's why she is on Washington Square that afternoon, and why she is demonstrating, with hundreds of other concerned citizens, against Senator McCarthy's abuse of human rights.

She is carrying a sign, as many other demonstrators on the Square are too. Holding it high above her head. A large rectangular piece of cardboard nailed to what looks like a broomstick. It proclaims, in handwritten letters, freedom of speech and freedom of political action. Moinous cannot read exactly what it says because the ink of the words is being washed away by the heavy downpour.

After they eventually meet, Moinous will question Sucette about her political activities, because he cannot understand why someone like her, someone so well off and so secure in her life-style, would want to get involved with other people's miseries, and Sucette will explain that it's because she is very concerned about what's happening in America. Dear love, you must understand that we live in a

strange period of history, and in a very sick world. Behind
our outrageous optimism and our glorified self-righteous-
ness lurks a dreadful absurdity. America may think it is the
guardian angel of the world right now, but thirty years from
now we, and I mean you and I darling, will have to account
for the stupidities of our time. The anxious, confused years
we are now living will lead us into tragic moments.

And Sucette will go on explaining, though Moinous will
ultimately discover all that for himself, years after he & Sucette have parted and he has learned to understand and
even question his adopted country, that America is a
chronically ailing society, but which believes, every dec-
ade or so, to have found a cure for its illness. The sicker it
gets, you see, the more it believes in its power of recupera-
tion and recovery. At the moments of high fever,
pseudophysicians appear everywhere and make history.
They become the doctors of the incurable. Frantic politi-
cians, demented military strategists, obsessed ideologists,
immunizing leaders, philosophical chiropractors, utopian
anaesthetists, they all examine the illness demagogically,
and the more incurable it is, the more they make believe
they have found a cure. They convulse in front of the patient, and the convulsions become contagious.

Sounds serious, Moinous says, shaking his head con-
cernedly. Yes, it is serious, Sucette continues, her face
glowing with excitement. In order for America to believe
in its national good health, it must be made to believe in
the existence of a germ which can be isolated and against
which it is possible to be inoculated for protection. And
so, periodically, America exposes such a germ, and
quickly offers a cure.

How do they do that? Moinous interrupts to show that he's still with Sucette.

Well, it's simple. Get rid of the spades, the spics, the spooks, the chinks, the coons, the colored, the niggers, the schwartzes. Burn the commies, the pinkos, the pansies, the jigs, the reds, the commie crapola, the liberals, the atheists. Lock up the gooks, the japs, the redskins, the weirdos, the black beauties, the bleeding hearts, the jungle bunnies, the dopies. Exterminate the freaks, the beatniks, the yids, the kikes, the hebes, the chosen people, the evolutionists. Oppress the meatheads, the dingbats, the dumbells, the hillbillies, the dumb polacks. Suppress the queers, the fairies, the lesbs, the fags, the queens, the fruits, the abnormals. Execute the four-eyes, the sheenies, the yanks, the rebs. Deport the dagos, the mics, the frogs, the krauts, the macaronis, the chicanos, and America will be healthy again.

Wow, that's incredible. Incredible. Moinous is so impressed with Sucette's diatribe, but especially with her amazing vocabulary, that he keeps repeating, Wow, that's incredible. And then he asks, Will you teach me all these American words?

Oh don't worry, Sucette replies, you'll learn them all soon enough. Especially how they are used to abuse one's fellowman. But now you understand why I have to get involved. Why I was demonstrating on Washington Square against that lunatic.

Indeed Moinous will understand and even witness, in the many years he will live in America, that all it takes is to create a scare, a red scare, a black scare, a youth scare, a yellow scare. All it takes is to fabricate a crisis. Any crisis. Economic, social, spiritual, ethnic, pathetic, anti-intellectual. And immediately America is on her way to a speedy recovery.

Strange paradox which Moinous cannot comprehend at first. But then Moinous is rather ignorant of the political situation in America at the time when he meets Sucette. He is too busy with his own survival to be involved in other people's misery. He simply lives out the consequences of politics as best he can. For if there is one question Moinous dreads and to which he has never been able to invent a satisfactory reply, it is the question, What the fuck am I doing here in the middle of all this?

And Moinous often asks this question of himself. Which means that he is not often happy with what he is doing and where he is doing it. Naturally, that question implies that Moinous would prefer to be doing something else, somewhere else. But even that something else, somewhere else, would probably elicit the same question from him. What the fuck am I doing here?

Therefore, on this dull, irksome afternoon, when Moinous wanders in the midst of all these shouting people gathered on Washington Square, he doesn't know about the demonstration, and is surprised to see this crowd. And especially all these policemen, some on foot, others on horseback, surround the place. What the hell is going on? Moinous wonders.

He came all the way down to the village to talk to his friend Charlie. The one-legged pigeon. That's what he calls him now. Charlie. Or Charlot, when he speaks French to him. For it seems that the one-legged pigeon, Charlie-Charlot, is a bilingual bird who responds just as well to French as to English.

In any case, Moinous comes all the way to Washington Square to see his friend Charlie because he has nothing better to do that afternoon since he's been fired from his last job. Not that it was the ideal job. Deliveryman for a dry cleaners on the East Side. Of course, that's not his profession. Just another job until something better and more permanent comes along. Moinous takes what he can get these days, since, according to the latest economic reports, there is a recession in America, and things will get worse, the newspapers are saying, before they get better.

Yet, in spite of all, there is a brighter and richer future ahead of him. And of course, there is also the eventual encounter with Sucette, which may perhaps lead to emotional involvement. For as Moinous will someday discover, in America the struggle for survival does not exist within the individual psyche alone, but within the collective unconsciousness of Capitalism. This discovery will not only help Moinous overcome and even forget the misery and loneliness of his early years in America, but also help him recuperate and perpetuate the dominant illusions of his youth. That's why America is called the land of opportunity.

And so, not only is there a more prosperous and happy future ahead of Moinous, but also a more intellectual, and perhaps even an artistic one. After all, he is not a dumb guy, even though he's been pushed around by fate, and by all sorts of unfortunate circumstances which are the cause of his present existential fiasco. No, Moinous is not dumb. On the contrary, bright, sensitive, full of energy, determined almost to the point of stubbornness, ambitious within the confines of reason, talented in many ways, even kind and generous on occasions.

The fundamental problem with Moinous is that he has never been able to function within the traditional rules of social behavior and decorum, and even if he were to become sufficiently confident to propose his own rules, he would soon be disobeying them as well. As a foreigner, Moinous is culturally and socially deprived.

As a matter of fact, that's exactly what one of his army buddies tells him one day when they are playing basketball. Shooting baskets for fun and relaxation in the gym at Fort Bragg where Moinous is stationed before being shipped overseas, and he keeps missing the hoop.

The problem with you, my man, the buddy says, a fast kid from New Jersey, is that you don't have the moves. As a frog who didn't get raised in this country, you are definitely deprived, culturally and socially, if you know what I mean.

Well it's because in France we don't play this fucking game, Moinous replies while piteously attempting another hook shot. You give me a soccer ball and I'll show you some moves.

And certainly, Moinous will have to go a long way before he learns the moves of the American-way-of-life. But what he needs right now is more class. More polish. Sophistication, in other words. And especially more education. Not experience. He's had plenty of that, even though he's only twenty-three years old. What Moinous needs is good solid intellectual and social education. And who knows, perhaps when Sucette begins to care for him after they come together, this will become possible.

For eventually, Moinous & Sucette may indeed come together, and that will have to be told, one way or another.
However, to describe now how their rapture gushes out
when finally they come together would be an impropriety.
It would probably sentimentalize that precious moment
and as a result vulgarize it. Too many love stories degener-
ate into cheap romances by being prematurely and super-
ficially described. It would be unfair to Moinous & Sucette
to turn their love affair into a mockery of itself.

Besides, right now, neither of them is concerned with
this question. Right now Sucette is demonstrating against
McCarthy with some measure of intensity and integrity,
while Moinous, jobless and depressed, stumbles into the
political gathering on Washington Square totally unaware
of what is going on. And of course, neither of them can anticipate what will unfold. For without expecting it, they
find themselves decoyed into a gratuitous exchange of
smiles which may not lead to anything, unless they talk to
each other.

Sucette will perhaps forget this brief incident when she
returns to her apartment and settles in for a quiet evening
with a good book. Probably the second volume of Franz
Kafka's *Diaries* which she has just received as a gift from
her friend Richard. Or else she will work on her short-
story assignment for the creative writing workshop she is
taking at Columbia University. The story is due in a couple
of weeks, and right now the plot is not going anywhere.
Perhaps she will make Moinous a character in that story.
Yes, a chance encounter for her heroine. That might make
something happen.

And by the time Moinous gets back to his furnished

room in the Bronx, just off the Grand Concourse, he too will forget the charming blonde who smiled at him so compassionately down in the Village, when he discovers that he's been evicted from his room for not having paid the rent in more than three weeks. The landlady threatened him several times these past few days.

Or else, even more depressed than earlier because of this new unfortunate turn of events, Moinous will build this chance encounter all out of proportion in his mind, and imagine himself already in love with this mysterious, beautiful woman. Yes, he will project into that smile the entire scenario of his love story. For indeed, one cannot write off the inequality between imagination and emotion in the mind of a lonely person.

Therefore, in spite of its rather problematic beginning, the love story of Moinous & Sucette will have to unfold, one way or another.

And if Moinous were familiar with Kafka's work, which regrettably he is not at this time, he would perhaps remember this marvelous passage from *The Diaries*, and quote it to himself to justify his present confusion. *The beginning of every story*, writes Kafka, *is ridiculous at first. There seems no hope that this newborn thing, still incomplete and tender in every joint, will be able to keep alive in the completed organization of the world, which, like every completed organization, strives to close itself off. However, one should not forget that the story, if it has any justification to exist, bears its complete organization within itself even before it has been fully formed. For this reason despair over the beginning of a story is unwarranted.*

T W O

Certainly neither Moinous nor Sucette should despair over the tentative beginning of their love story. For despite the missed opportunity on Washington Square, things will perhaps work out for them eventually, even if Sucette, now back in her apartment trying to decide how she'll spend the evening—either reading or writing, has already forgotten the incident, and Moinous, out of job, broke, and depressed, is on his way to his shabby furnished room in the Bronx, by subway, to discover he's been evicted, and therefore becomes distracted from his sentimental reveries, at least for the time being.

He was right about his premonition. When he arrives in the Bronx and goes up the stairs to the third floor of his building, Moinous finds his suitcase, the same beat-up black cardboard suitcase with which he arrived in America five years earlier, and the rest of his belongings piled in the hallway, and a note thumbtacked on the door of his room. NO MONEY NO ROOM SORRY. The landlady has thrown his stuff out into the corridor and changed the lock on the door. And so once again Moinous is out in the cold.

What to do now? At most three dollars left to his name, as noted earlier. Even less now since, on his way home, Moinous stops at Nedicks for a quick hot dog and an orange drink, and has to buy a subway token. And nothing, nothing in sight. Where can he go? Where, with his suitcase into which his landlady has shoved his belongings?

Moinous doesn't really have a friend, an acquaintance, or anyone like that, he can call and to whom he can say,

Hey look, I've got a problem. I've just been kicked out of my apartment. I need a place to stay for a couple of nights. You know, until I find something else. I'll sleep on your couch. Or even on the floor of your living room. Just for a few days.

No, Moinous doesn't know anyone like that. Even the army buddies, those who promised to stay in touch after they got out, have faded away. He has no friends in New York. Except for Charlie, the one-legged pigeon. But that bird is no solution for his present dilemma. What Moinous needs now is not animal friendship but human compassion. And anyway, it's too cold to sleep on a bench in the middle of Washington Square like a pigeon. Especially at this time of year. In March. Or February.

As he sits on the steps of the staircase across from the locked door of his furnished room contemplating the situation, Moinous doesn't really feel sorry for himself because he's been evicted and has no one to turn to. Since coming to America, he's learned to live with hardship, and to endure his loneliness without tumbling into self-pity at every misfortune. Ah yes, loneliness, for which Moinous discovered there is no equivalent word in his native French. *Isolement. Solitude. Sentiment d'abandon.* These are the words he found in the little bilingual pocket-size dictionary he always carried with him during the first months when he still struggled with the language. Perhaps the French are never lonely. They only have feelings of abandonment. Bullshit, Moinous thinks. He could tell them something about loneliness in America.

Yet, in spite of all, Moinous rarely indulges in self-pity. Just because his emotions are sometimes boggled does not mean that he gives up on the human condition. Moinous is a stubborn optimist. But right now he's facing a serious problem. No place to go and no one to help him.

Ah, if only he had spoken to the charming blonde who smiled at him earlier that afternoon.

Moinous becomes acutely aware of his aloneness in New York when he comes home one day to his room in the Bronx. Two or three weeks before he & Sucette smile at each other. In fact, the very day he's fired from his job at the dry cleaners. And the landlady, Madame la Concierge, as he likes to call her, rushes after him as he goes up the stairs.

Hey Mister Moinous, Mister Moinous, there's a letter here for you.

A letter? Moinous is intrigued because he never receives any mail. And for good reason, since he never writes to anyone. Except during his first few months in America when he still wrote letters to old friends or even to some distant cousins back in France. But after a while he stopped writing since there was nothing new or nothing important to say. And they did too, the old friends and distant cousins. Then there was the stretch in the army. Two wasted years. And besides, who has time to write letters when you're fighting the war in Korea, or doing black market in Tokyo. Too busy or too tired all the time.

No, Moinous never receives any mail. Unless it's a letter that reaches him by mistake. A wrong address, or else the right address but the wrong name, which often happens when you live in the Bronx. This time, however, the letter his landlady hands him is really addressed to him. It is his name there, neatly written on the envelope. Moinous has a strange feeling in his stomach. To receive a letter, just like that out of the blue, gives Moinous the same feeling of anguish others get when they receive a telegram.

He takes the letter from the landlady, holds it with two timid fingers, looks at it but without opening it as he feels his Adam's apple rise in his throat.

In his room, he stares at the letter, trying to guess what's in it as he sits on his only chair. For even though the newspaper ad which led him to this room in the Bronx, six months earlier, when he got out of the army, clearly stated, PLEASANT FULLY FURNISHED STUDIO APARTMENT, ALL COMFORT, Moinous discovered after he moved in that in fact the room was rather sordidly furnished, and the comfort greatly overstated. But then it will take some time, and some further frustrating disappointments, for Moinous to learn that in America misrepresentation is the standard way for the system to function and perpetuate itself.

He walks into the room, six months earlier. Sets down his black suitcase in the middle of the floor, trying to catch his breath after the three flights of stairs. Looks around and sees that the so-called furniture consists of a narrow bed, a Murphy that drops down from the wall out of a closet, with a gray-stained mattress, a pillow that feels like a sack full of sand, a little square table with a broken leg, and only one chair, which suggests that guests are not welcome in this place, a torn, faded piece of flowered rug thrown on the floor between the bed and the table, and in one corner of the room a sink, next to which stands a small electric burner on a cracked lacquered shelf, the kitchen in other words. As for the toilet, it's down the hall, and the shower across from it. Moinous sneers dejectedly at the pitiful naturalism of his new home.

So he sits there on his one chair, two or three weeks before his eviction, still holding the mysterious letter in his hand. Finally, he tears one corner, slides his finger inside the envelope and rips it open. He begins to read. *This chain letter of luck*, it says on a sheet of heavy-grain paper, *was sent to me and I am sending it to you twenty-four hours after reception as instructed. The one who breaks this chain will surely be victim of extreme bad luck. For instance, Miss Rachel Ploth was found suffocating in her apartment in Queens two days after she broke the chain, and a certain Mr. Schlock broke both his legs in a bicycle accident soon after he too broke the chain. So don't take a chance. Keep this chain going. Keep luck flowing. Act immediately. All you have to do is make TWENTY COPIES of this letter and send it to TWENTY OF YOUR FRIENDS OR ACQUAINT-ANCES within TWENTY-FOUR HOURS after you've received it, and luck will smile upon you instantly.*

The signature at the bottom of the letter is undecipherable, at least to Moinous. Simon, or Samuel, or perhaps Sylvia. The first letter is an S for sure, but the rest totally unreadable. In any case, there is no one Moinous knows by these names. But what an unexpected sign. Just when Moinous is so depressed because he's been fired from his job. It makes him feel good to know that someone out there wishes him luck. Surely his fortune is about to take a lucky turn. He feels it. Only in America, he thinks.

His heart pounding with excitement, Moinous rereads the letter. But then it occurs to him, to whom can he send this lucky letter? He would like to mail the letter to twenty people to bring them luck, for once that luck is passing his way, and he can share it with others who may also need it. And of course, profit himself from this lucky message. But he doesn't know that many people. Such is the sad condition of his present life.

Nonetheless, Moinous takes out a piece of paper and a pencil and starts a list. He is still wearing his overcoat as he sits at the table since it is a rather cold evening and there isn't much heat in his furnished room. In fact, on cold winter nights Moinous often sleeps with his overcoat on, a gray raglan tweed he bought in Klein's basement for his first winter in America. He was so proud of that coat when it was new. It made him look almost like a real American. But now it's a little worn. Doesn't matter. Moinous is excited about the chain letter.

However, after he has written the name of his landlady, Mrs. Mary Connolly, and that of his boss, Mr. Marcus Gross, at the dry cleaning store on Lexington Avenue where Moinous works, or rather where he used to work, since he's now been fired, and also the name of the other fellow who works there, the guy who does the pressing, Joe Kocieniewski, even though he doesn't like him very much because he's a wise guy who thinks he's king shit, but what the hell, perhaps he too needs a bit of luck, after he has written these three names neatly on the sheet of paper, Moinous cannot think of anyone else to whom he can pass on this message of good fortune.

Now were he to receive this lucky letter the day he smiles at Sucette on Washington Square, and of course speak to her, then go with her for coffee to become acquainted, Moinous would certainly add her name to his list. But that's useless speculation since Moinous gets the chain letter of luck two or three weeks before he & Sucette bump into each other on that rainy afternoon. Two or three weeks before his eviction, in other words.

It seems that Moinous is never in the right place at the right time. Or else if he happens to be in the right place at the right time, he does not seem to recognize the opportunity offered to him, and therefore fails to grab it. Perhaps this is because he has not yet learned to take the kinds of chances most real Americans take with their go-get-it attitude.

Moinous rereads the three names he has written on his piece of paper and thinks hard while biting on the eraser at the tip of his pencil. He even writes the names a second time. But these are the only three people he knows right now. He cannot say they are his friends, but he is willing to send them the letter. Everybody needs luck in life, he says aloud. But then he wonders if by sending only three letters instead of the required twenty he will perhaps be going against the rules of the letter and break the chain. It does say specifically, in bold letters, MAKE TWENTY COPIES and send them to TWENTY PEOPLE. Right there on the sheet of paper Moinous is holding in his hand. For a moment he contemplates adding his name to the list and sending one, or even several of the letters to himself. But this may also be against the rules of the lucky chain, and may in fact cause him infinite bad luck since the letter would only be going in circles. No good. And even with his name on the list, he still needs sixteen more. Or let's say a dozen if he writes his name five times. To list himself more than that would really be defying luck.

It is not easy to deal with luck, particularly when it comes unexpectedly. It seems that for Moinous everything, good luck as well as bad, happens in the rigamarole of contrariety. Yet, in his eagerness to keep the chain going, he begins to wander in circles in his mind in search of more names. But he cannot think of any other names. Or when after deep probing, a name finally flashes to his mind in a vague mental blur, like the name of an army buddy with whom he fought the war in Korea, or that of another buddy with whom he was involved in black marketing in Tokyo, or even, reaching deeper, that of an old childhood friend or a distant cousin back in France, it remains either a first name with a forgotten last name, or a last name for which Moinous has no address.

Moinous lost the little address book he used to carry in his pocket when he first came to America. A black one with an imitation leather cover. He lost it just before he got out of the army. Actually, he threw it into the Pacific Ocean one stormy night as he stood defiantly on the bridge of the navy tub which was taking him, and thousands of other G.I.s who had served in the Far East, back home to be discharged.

It was, no doubt, a romantic gesture, but one which Moinous performed symbolically that night. Let's call it the unfathomable longing of the soul to vex itself and violate its own nature. For at that moment, with the wind blowing in his face, and the waves crashing against the hull of the ship, Moinous decided to cut himself off from the past now that he was returning home to his adopted country to resume civilian life.

His first two years in America, before he was drafted

into the army, had been disasterous on all counts. Poverty, humiliation, hunger, unemployment, loneliness. Moinous endured all that during those two years. Plus, of course, the chaotic burden of his obsessive memories. But this time it would be different. Especially with the two-hundred-and-fifty-dollar-mustering-out pay they were going to give him at Fort Dix. A new life. Yes, a fresh start. That's what Moinous thought when he hurled his address book into the ocean. He had matured out there in the fox-holes of Korea. Now he would meet new people. Different and interesting kinds of people. Now he would escape the vicious circles of bad luck. Perhaps even fall in love.

As he stares at the three names on his sheet of paper, and searches his mind for other names to add to the list, once again Moinous confronts his pathetic aloneness and the emptiness of his present condition. And of course, also confronts the inescapable unlucky consequences of having to break the chain letter, simply because he does not know twenty people. He is almost on the verge of tears when suddenly he has an idea. A terrific idea.

He rushes out of his room, down the stairs, into the street, runs to the nearest public telephone booth. For obviously there is no telephone in his room. Whom could Moinous call? And who would call him? But what a tremendous idea. Standing in the booth, he eagerly adds to his list names of people and their addresses out of the phone book. Flipping the pages at random. Pointing to a name with his finger, his eyes closed. Perhaps that's how the person who sent him the letter got his name. No, that's not possible, because Moinous is not listed in the telephone book. Ah, doesn't matter. Twenty friends or acquaintances, the chain letter says. Well, everybody in the phone book is a potential friend or acquaintance.

Moinous has already written six or seven names on his sheet of paper when he suddenly stops. He's just realized that in order to mail the twenty letters he will need to buy some stationery. Twenty sheets of paper and twenty envelopes. And of course, twenty stamps. He calculates. The stamps alone will cost sixty cents. This is the time of the three-cent stamp. At least thirty-nine cents, maybe more, for the pad of paper, depending on the quality he chooses. For a lucky letter one cannot be too cheap. Another forty-nine cents for the envelopes. All in all close to a buck and a half. No, Moinous cannot afford this kind of expense. Not at this time, when he is without a job. And nothing in sight. Nothing. Moinous leans on his elbows on top of the telephone book and holds his head between his hands. Of course, if he sacrifices that dollar and a half to send the letters, out of the little money he has left to survive, perhaps luck will smile upon him. Perhaps he will find another job immediately. Even meet someone who will bring him happiness. But that's taking a great deal of risk, and Moinous is in no frame of mind right now to gamble on such uncertainties.

He steps out of the phone booth. Stands on the sidewalk for a moment still debating the issue with himself. Finally he walks slowly back to his furnished room, feeling the gloom of loneliness descend upon him. Just before entering his building, he tears the chain letter and his partial list into little bits and throws them into the gutter.

Now, as he sits on the steps of the staircase across the hall from his locked room, the one from which he's been evicted, Moinous realizes how alone he is. And also how the broken chain letter, two or three weeks earlier, may have been the cause of his present streak of bad luck. For a moment he considers going downstairs to argue with Mrs. Connolly. Even plead with her to let him stay a few more days. Until he finds another job. But Moinous is not the type of person who begs for favors. He has his pride, like anyone else. That much can be said for him. He may have been humiliated time after time in his unfortunate life, but he will not get down on his knees to beg. No man should ever kneel before another man, or woman, he says aloud, throwing his head back, neither to pray nor to beg. He picks up his suitcase resolutely and walks out of the building.

It is late evening now. Past ten o'clock. The suitcase is heavy. And of course, it's raining. Icy rain. But Moinous should not despair, even though he is broke, jobless, and now homeless. He has a blind date with love. He doesn't know it yet, but soon the indomitable obsessiveness of love will come bursting upon him.

But before that. Before entering the absolute seizure of that moment. Before falling into the whirlwind of passion, as the saying goes. Moinous must find a place to spend the night, and decide what he will do to get himself out of his present dilemma.

First a job. Yes, he must find a job. Any damn thing to keep his life going. His life? What a joke. Moinous often thinks of his life as a joke in progress, or of something already finished, even though he's only twenty-three years old. And yet, every time his life seems to come to an end, something happens to give him hope again.

As he goes down the stairs into the subway at the Grand Concourse entrance, he curses himself for not having spoken to the charming blonde.

If only Moinous could imagine away the material nuisances of his life and concentrate on its emotional aspects, he might free himself of the illusions of having to succeed in America. But being young and imperfect, he goes on searching for his place, even if the prospects for positive nondelusionary hope are all out, and he keeps on stumbling over his own misfortunes.

Therefore, he knows that in the morning he will again be on the jobpath. After another tormented night. Again be standing in line with the ad section of *The New York Times* tucked under his arm, in which he has circled a dozen or so help wanted ads. No experience necessary, that goes without saying. Usually these jobs don't last very long, but they keep you going. And hoping too before crumbling into despair again. Ah yes, hope and despair, that inseparable couple, as Moinous explains to Sucette, during an evening of hopeless discussion about Moinous's future. Hope, the hole ahead that we try to fill or fulfill. And despair, the hole we leave behind.

Since he's been discharged from the army, and soon after he spent his two-hundred-and-fifty-dollar-mustering-out pay on a few necessary items of clothing, two new pairs of pants, a sport coat, four shirts, a pair of shoes, socks, and underwear, lucky for him he kept his old raglan tweed coat while in the service, in other words, the essentials to be a civilian again and be presentable, Moinous has had sixteen of these temporary jobs, which causes him to realize more and more how erratic, skittish, discontinuous, monstrously disappointing life in America is. Making it also impossible for Moinous to know if he is cornered in a socio-economic impasse, or if in fact he is forging ahead. Nonetheless, he persists in his search for a place in life as he goes from one job to another.

The delivery job at the dry cleaners lasted only two weeks. Before that he worked for a carpet-cleaning outfit in upper Manhattan. Making house calls. Or rather apartment calls in the neighborhood. Moinous was dismissed when he got fresh, yes that's how it was reported to his boss, fresh, with the lady whose carpet he was shampooing as best he could.

That's not true, she's lying, Moinous told his boss. She's the one who made a pass at me while I was on my knees scrubbing her filthy rug. She kept getting down on the floor next to me and throwing her boobs at me. So I grabbed one of them. Big deal. I'm human too.

Moinous doesn't always grasp the subtle meaning of female gestures. Not that he is naive. Perhaps too overanxious and unceremonious, is how Sucette puts it to him later on when he tries to rush things with her. It gets him into trouble. Especially since the female psyche often appears to him as a heap of deceptions. In any event, he is immediately fired from the carpet-cleaning outfit.

Luckily he gets the delivery job with the dry cleaners a couple of days later. On a Thursday, by pure chance. A sign in the window of the store on Lexington Avenue, uptown, where Moinous happens to be walking that afternoon. For no specific reasons. Just bumming around. He has already stood in line with his *New York Times* want ads for five hours that morning trying to land something. But it was hopeless.

He was too late for the dishwasher job at the deli on Seventh Avenue. They hired the third guy in line, and Moinous was eleventh. At five-thirty in the morning. Sonofabitch. The night watchman in a furniture store on Third Avenue appealed to him because of the hours. Moinous doesn't mind working at night. On the contrary, it prevents him from having sleepless nights. But again no luck. They wanted experience, and especially someone tougher-looking than Moinous. Then after that, way on the East Side, there was the doorman for a luxurious apartment building. That would have been nice. They found him too young. And besides, the uniform they had him try on was too big. Fuck them, Moinous said to himself as he walked away from the swanky building.

Later he has a hamburger and a cup of coffee in one of those standup joints near Grand Central Station, and then wanders up Lexington Avenue. That's how he notices the sign in the window of the dry cleaners. No experience needed, it says. He goes in to inquire and Mr. Gross puts him to work on the spot since he's way behind in his deliveries and the customers are complaining.

Not a bad job. You're not stuck inside. You meet people. Some of them very friendly. Mostly housewives because the husbands are at work during delivery hours. Sometimes they invite you in for a cup of coffee or something. Tell you their stories. Complain about how life is boring. Show you the kids' pictures who are in school. Ask about your life. Notice your French accent, and immediately tell you how charming and sexy it is. In fact, that's how Moinous got into trouble again.

This lady, middle thirties, quite gorgeous and sexy, opens the door and says, Come on in, come on in. Just hang the cleaning in that closet. She's wearing a light-blue negligee, full-length. Sort of transparent. Moinous can see the tips of her breasts through the fabric. You wait here a minute, she says, I'll get your money. The lady disappears into another room. Moinous is standing in the middle of the living room admiring the fancy furniture in this elegant apartment on 86th Street between Madison and Park. He looks at the paintings on the wall. Mostly landscapes. Must be originals, he thinks. Feels the thickness and plushness of the carpet with his feet. He learned to appreciate carpets on his last job. The lady, ravishing red hair loose over her shoulders, green eyes, freckled skin, a real tigress, returns and her negligee is half open now, showing her lovely thighs almost up to her crotch, and one of her tits is exposed, and Moinous understands this to be a signal. She moves closer to him, all perfumed, and starts giggling. You're quite a handsome young man, aren't you? Moinous blushes. She's holding a twenty-dollar bill in her hand. You can keep the change, she says. But instead of taking the money and saying Thank you very much, Moinous grabs the sexy lady. She screams, What the hell do you think you're doing, young man? Even though she's pulling him toward her while pushing him away at the same time. So hard in fact, they both stagger and fall to the floor, knocking over a chair. Looks like an antique chair. They roll on top of each other on the carpet. Wall to wall, pure wool, Moinous notices. She's on top of him now, still shouting between her clenched teeth, You little bastard. One of her legs is forcing its way between Moinous's thighs, and he feels her nails in his shoulder. Moinous panics. He struggles and manages to sneak out from underneath this wild woman, gets up, runs to the door, down the stairs, even though the apartment is on the 37th floor. Naturally, he forgets to take the money. By the time he gets back to the store, the lady has already telephoned to report his insolent conduct, and he's fired on the spot.

That's how it goes for Moinous, always victim of his own innocence. Not that he's irresponsible or careless. But he's young, and not too experienced in the American-way-of-things. He's been in America five years, true, but the two-year stretch in the army sort of messed up the continuity of his social assimilation.

So again he's out of a job, and now evicted from his furnished room. And since there is a recession, it will not be easy for him to find another job. He's not proud. He'll take anything. He'll wait in line again every morning with his newspaper, but he knows that by the time his turn comes the job will already be gone, or they'll find some reason for not hiring him. That's what has been happening these past two or three weeks. So he spends his days wandering around the city without any purpose, and that's how he gets to Washington Square, that rainy afternoon, and accidentally bumps into Sucette during the anti-McCarthy demonstration.

They smile at each other. Nothing unusual about that. But they do not speak. How dumb of me not to have spoken to her, Moinous reflects as he sits in the rattling subway car, his suitcase squeezed between his legs. He's on his way downtown to try to find a place to spend the night. Maybe she would have given him her phone number. He could call her now. Explain his unfortunate situation, and she would invite him over, and who knows, yes who knows what would happen after that.

It is at that very moment, when Sucette's smiling face flashes in his mind and the lights flicker in the subway, that Moinous realizes he's fallen in love, even though he knows nothing about Sucette, not even her name. Unbelievable. Just because of a smile. Yet, it is not that preposterous. Many great loves of the past were initiated by little more than a conniving smile.

By the time Moinous gets off the subway at Times Square, and stands in front of the window display of a sporting goods store, absentmindedly looking at the tennis rackets, the golf clubs, the canoes, the sexy sun tanned mannequins in bathing suits, he feels an immense sadness come over him. No, not sadness, but a kind of hollowness in his bones, as if the marrow is oozing out, and the bones are weeping. It is, of course, the most ancient sob in the history of man. And suddenly, he knows. He feels it. Hears it in his bones. Moinous is in love.

How stupid. How idiotic. Just because a girl, a woman, smiles at you. But Sucette's smile is not just the kind that says, Oh-excuse-me-for-being-so-clumsy. No, it is a smile that says, Oh-please-talk-to-me. For that day, as in the past several months, in spite of her involvement in politics, Sucette is also suffering the anguish of her loneliness. Unfortunately, Moinous is not very good at deciphering smiles. Nor are his own smiles very precise in their intent.

Ah *merde, merde alors,* I'm in love, he murmurs. Moinous often speaks bilingually to himself when he is confused. As he walks east on 42nd Street toward Grand Central Station where he has decided to spend the night, in the waiting room, he projects himself forward into his love for Sucette. He feels in his bones the intensity of its hope, the gushing of its passion, the rapture of its bliss, but also the fury of its conditional disappointment. For as soon as a love story begins it has already begun to end, though right now Moinous is not ready to imagine that ending.

He sees himself in Sucette's apartment. He knows it is charming, cozy, and intimate. In the dim light of the alcove where the bed is located, he sees himself watching Sucette undress. Ah, how lovely. How her loveliness is revealed so artlessly. He lights a Gauloise. Asks Sucette to undress again. And again. And again, as the two of them giggle their happiness, unaware of the panic inherent in the sensual gestures to come. He presses his head to her bosom, and breathes heavily. Sucette strokes his hair and whispers tender words in his ear.

Before this moment, Sucette had been miserable but reasonable. Now she is happy and demented. The months of frustration and suppressed desire peel off with every piece of clothing she drops on the floor. Her unbridled babble gives evidence of her wild irrationality. Oh, I want you, I want you so much, she whimpers. Moinous kisses the tiny birthmark between her breasts. He touches her soft pale skin. She caresses his back. Squeezes the muscles of his shoulder. His fingers search her pubic hair. It is sparse and golden. She pulls him toward the bed. Turns off the light. In the relapse of darkness they tumble into the abyss of vertigo to reach that grandiose infinity where desire is appeased. Suddenly a great commotion immobilizes Sucette in her center of gravity, and for Moinous four years, eleven months, and two days of solitude come to an end.

A gust of wind blows icy rain in Moinous's face and forces him to take refuge in a doorway across from the New York Public Library, at the corner of 42nd Street and Fifth Avenue. He wipes the rain off his face with his hand. How stupid of me not to talk to her. Who knows. Who knows where I would be spending the night.

Without going that far, it would be sad for Moinous if in that unscandalized mess of his life he could not achieve a little happiness. Exchange a smile with a woman like Sucette. Perhaps a few words. Yes, a smile and a few affectionate words to carry away with him to his loneliness. That is not asking too much.

And so, as he waits out the heavy downpour in the doorway, Moinous wanders further ahead into time. He now sees himself, crushed by despair, walking away from Sucette's apartment, his black suitcase in his hand, their love story having reached its conditional disappointment. That too is inevitable. For Moinous has learned to resign himself to the fact that everything that happens to him, good or bad, is his life.

It may not be possible to describe Moinous & Sucette's love affair in detail, even though in most love stories concentration on irrelevant details is a way of avoiding melodrama and sentimentality, for it is difficult nowadays to speak of love. Difficult to speak words of love without corrupting them, without polluting them with clichés. Yet, one way or another, Moinous & Sucette will meet. They will fall in love, and ultimately consume their desire, in spite of the fragile organism of their existence.

That's how the story of Moinous & Sucette progresses. Tentatively and confusedly at first. But then most love stories are usually messy in the beginning, and disastrous at the end. Somehow the middle always settles into quieter moments.

But the story of Moinous & Sucette is so unpredictable, and so full of ups and downs. Certainly not the typical romantic love story. That's for sure. More the ubiquitous type. Yet full of tenderness. Tenderness and irony, the marks of their emotional involvement.

They meet on Washington Square. Or rather, almost meet there, as previously established. Two weeks later, by pure chance, they'll probably come face to face again, but this time they speak to each other, and become acquainted. Moinous is immediately attracted by Sucette's passive but avid manner, and she by the vagueness and candor of his gaze. Over their first cups of coffee together they talk about their lives in New York City.

They love New York even though neither is a native of the city. They discover that they are both urban types. Big-city people. Therefore, no excessive rural digressions enter their story, within the confines of their restless relationship. No weeping willows and stormy lakes, tormented skies and inflamed sunsets to commiserate with them. No exhausted horns of the moon, nor grievous birds through verdurous glooms and winding mossy ways. None of that anthropomorphic whiny flora and fauna.

In fact, Moinous often says to Sucette, later when they are living together and she proposes a walk in the country or a picnic in the park, that nature leaves him indifferent. This because at one time he was too close to it when he worked on the farm for three years during the war. I hated it. I was just a boy then, and let me tell you, it was tough, he explains to Sucette, really tough. Especially for someone like me who had been raised in a quiet neighborhood in Paris without ever doing any hard work, except going to school. But that's another story, with little relevance to the present situation. Though Sucette will want to know more about that period of his life when they become intimate, particularly since Moinous always seems reluctant to speak about his parents, and what happened to them during the war.

Sucette, on the other hand, likes nature, within reason. Long solitary walks in the country. In autumn especially, when the trees turn technicolor and try to imitate impressionist paintings. That's how she puts it to Moinous one October day as they walk hand in hand in Central Park. I like to be surrounded by colorful vegetation, she says. It gives me a feeling of calmness.

Sucette always has fresh flowers on the table, and exotic plants in the windows of her apartment. She even keeps a philodendron in her bathroom. Makes it more pleasant and livable in there, she says, and besides, the humidity helps it grow. But when Moinous eventually moves in with her, he often complains that the damn thing gets in his way whenever he needs to use the bathroom. He keeps bumping his head on the pot above the toilet. It's a small bathroom. Typical of New York apartments. One of those converted old brownstones, on 105th Street, off Riverside Drive.

Yet in spite of all this vegetation in her apartment, and her occasional escapes into nature, Sucette is a city person. And quite sophisticated. Which is understandable with her Boston background. New England from way back. Perhaps as far back as the *Mayflower*. At least, that's what my folks claim, she tells Moinous during one of their moments of self-revelation. Yes, I am a twelfth-generation American, can you believe that. A perfect white Anglo-Saxon Protestant. Which means that I have to endure all the standard social and moral implications of such a background. And the frustrations too. Sucette tries hard, though often in vain, as Moinous will have occasion to witness, to escape these implications and frustrations.

You see, she explains after the disastrous weekend in Boston, a good name and wealth do not necessarily make for understanding people. My family can no longer distinguish the essential from the superficial. Like most upper-middle-class Americans, they have lost sight of their dreams and ideals. This is why, from the day I ran away from home to be on my own, I got involved in moral causes, and even in radical politics. You could say that it's a way for me to react against my background, even if sometimes I doubt the efficacity of political action.

Reason, therefore, for Sucette's participation in the anti-McCarthy demonstration on Washington Square the day she & Moinous bump into each other. During the Cold War. At the peak of the red scare. That's when Moinous & Sucette exchange smiles, and subsequently become emotionally involved. Certainly not the best time for falling in love. But then lovers do not often synchronize their emotions with historical events.

As a matter of fact, their accidental encounter occurs a few months before Joe McCarthy is forced to resign from the Senate as a result of public outrage. Moinous & Sucette smile at each other on March 15, 1954. Exactly two months to the day before Moinous's 23rd birthday, on May 15. Which he celebrates with Sucette. By then they are quite intimate. For his birthday, Sucette gives Moinous a sweater. A really superb beige cashmere which she buys at Brooks Brothers.

Joe McCarthy is formally condemned, for conduct contrary to Senate traditions, by a vote of *sixty-seven yeas to twenty-two nays*, on December 2, 1954. By a happy coincidence, the same day Sucette is celebrating her birthday. She is thirty-two years old, nine years older than Moinous.

The two of them are rejoicing as they discuss the vote of the Senate. Personally, Sucette declares in an outburst of passion, I would have thrown the bastard in jail.

Me, I would have stoned him publicly and then deported him to a desert island, Moinous retorts, remembering Napoleon's plight. Under Sucette's influence he has gained political awareness.

They toast the decision of the Senate, and Sucette's birthday too. They are in the middle of dinner. A candlelight tête-à-tête in Sucette's apartment. She has prepared an elaborate and delicious French meal for the occasion. Escargots, coq au vin, salade d'endives, and for dessert a mousse au chocolat. Moinous takes charge of buying the wine. A superb St. Emilion 1951. As a Frenchman he has a natural instinct for good wines.

That's the best present I could get, Sucette says. To see

that raving demagogue finally exposed and kicked out of office. I worked so hard to see this day.

Forget the sonofabitch and let's enjoy your birthday, Moinous says as he leans over the table to kiss Sucette. She holds his head between her hands as their mouths meet.

Do you realize I'm thirty-two years old today, she says as they sit back in their chairs and her face suddenly turns somber. And I'm beginning to look it. That means nine years older than you. Isn't it amazing how the two of us manage to get along so well in spite of our age difference? I really don't understand what you find in me that pleases you.

You're the nicest, kindest person I've ever met, Moinous replies. You're so good to me. And then, almost as an afterthought, you don't look thirty-two, you know. You're beautiful.

Nonetheless, the age difference is crucial to their relationship. And also the conflicting aspects of their zodiacal signs. Not the most perfect match, according to the stars. Moinous, of course, a Taurus. A typical bull with his feet on the ground and his head in the clouds who struggles constantly to conquer vanity and indolence. And so insecure, even when things are going well for him. Sucette, like a true Sagittarian, delves into hidden truths and indulges in endless introspection. She is concerned with spiritual wisdom and political knowledge. Economically protected by some mysterious twist of fate, she understands the value of silence and solitude. She never hastens into decisions, for she knows it creates complications. She has learned to live alone and to like it. No wonder it takes a while for her to allow Moinous to penetrate her privacy.

After he meets Sucette again, at the Librairie Française, and after they go for coffee together, Moinous sees Sucette regularly. He often visits her in her apartment. But their conflicting personalities and the age difference cause many anguishing moments in their relationship. For more than a month and a half, forty-two days to be precise, since Moinous counts the days with mounting fervor, she resists his obvious and bullish sexual advances. Moinous is not very subtle when it comes to sexual advances, and does not understand how easily the female psyche can be wounded. Utterly frustrated, he projects his desire with hysterical infantilism.

Sucette's resistance puzzles him. Moinous does not think of himself as a great seducer. He's too timid for that. But those few sexual experiences he's had so far in his life never took that long to reach the point of total oblivion. Of course, Moinous has never been in love before, at least not the way he feels it now. Nevertheless, he cannot comprehend why a woman like Sucette, so mature, so independent, is afraid to commit herself to sexual bliss. Especially since she keeps asking him to come over to her place, and they sit there, late into the night, talking, laughing, and even fondling each other.

One night, some three weeks into their relationship, Moinous asks Sucette why she keeps turning him down. And she replies, Look, I like you, I like you very much. I think you're a great guy. But I'm not ready to fall into bed with you, that's all.

And Moinous asks naively, Why? Is it because I'm

younger than you? Or because I'm not good enough for you?

No, you fool. It has nothing to do with age or anything like that. It s just difficult for me to explain. That's the way I am. Be patient. When you know me better you'll understand.

The gradual meltdown of moral absolutes in Sucette has opened in her the gate to ambivalence and indecision. And so while she tries to keep a cool classic equipoise during those forty-two days of self-denial, Moinous shakes off sparks as he acts out a one-man melodrama of insecurity, anxiety, and diffidence, even though Sucette keeps telling him that in matters of love one must have principles.

During that time Moinous goes literally crazy with frustration, wasted desire, and self-doubt. Often, after he leaves Sucette's apartment, late at night, he stands for hours in the street, staring miserably at her window, even after the light goes out. Then, feeling dejected and rejected, he walks aimlessly in the streets of the city, not even caring about his own safety, his hair and face drenched with rain, the crease in his pants washed away.

Sometimes he walks all the way down to Washington Square just to see his friend Charlie, the one-legged pigeon, and tell him about his misery. But Charlie is not always there in the middle of the night. Perhaps he too has his own sentimental problems. It must be complicated for a one-legged pigeon to make out with the female members of his own species.

Sometimes Moinous calls Sucette from some telephone booth and begs her to let him come back.

My poor Moinous, you're so childish. What am I going

to do with you? She says trying to comfort him. Where are you? Do you realize what time it is? It's almost morning. Go home. Go home. I'll see you tomorrow.

According to Freud, some obstacle is necessary to swell the tide of the libido to its height. But forty-two days?

That's how long Sucette holds Moinous at bay, and all the while he keeps wondering if perhaps there's something wrong with him. He even blames his failure to connect with Sucette on the fact that he is a foreigner with little experience of American women. After all, most of his sexual adventures occurred in the Far East with Orientals. Japanese and Korean prostitutes. He wonders if he will always remain a clumsy foreigner. A failure as the classic French lover. Or if someday he will be able to embody all the legendary aspects of the contemporary American male, especially as depicted in the Hollywood movies Moinous saw before he came to America.

Yes, he wonders if he too can become sexy and heroic. Casual and forceful. Tough and unyielding. Adored and admired for his strength and fortitude, even if it means becoming desperate and psychotic as a result.

Of course, all this happens much later. And only if Moinous & Sucette meet again. Right now Moinous is walking on 42nd Street with his suitcase in his hand. The rain has let up a bit. He arrives at Grand Central Station. The great hall of the terminal is deserted. The last train has left. Ah how marvelous it would be to take a train and go. Go anywhere. Just to get the hell out of this damn city. But of course Moinous could not afford to buy a ticket. And where would he go?

Five or six people have settled in for the night in the

waiting room. A young couple occupies one of the wooden benches. The young man is asleep sitting up, his head propped against a canvas bag, his female companion curled up on the bench, her head resting on his lap. She is covered with a raincoat. Maybe they missed their train. Moinous walks past their bench trying not to look at them. He feels embarrassed. On another bench, an old man wrapped in newspapers is snoring loudly. Probably a drunk snore. Far at one end of the waiting room, a woman in disheveled clothes is talking aloud to herself. Moinous notices the purple varicose veins on her bare legs, and the black umbrella she holds squeezed between her thighs. She gives him an ugly toothless smile as he walks by. Moinous blushes and looks away. There may be one or two more people stretched on some of the other benches, but Moinous cannot see them, he only senses their wretched presence. He feels like walking out of this place, ashamed that he might be taken for one of these derelicts.

He goes to the farthest bench, away from the entrance. Sits down. His suitcase at his feet. He assumes the attitude of someone who is waiting for a train. He keeps glancing up at the clock above the entrance door. It's cold in the waiting room. There is a draft. He hunches his shoulders forward, pulls the collar of his overcoat up around his ears, and pushes his hands deep into the pockets. He could open his suitcase and take out his old sweater, but he doesn't want to draw attention to himself. And yet, lately, he's been so weak for lack of decent food, and all that wandering in the rain, he catches cold in his dreams.

He isn't sleepy, but a little hungry. He takes out his

money and counts it. One dollar bill and thirty-seven cents in change. He tries to remember what he spent since he left his furnished room early in the morning to look for a job. The hot dog, the orange drink, three cups of coffee. Or was it four? The egg salad sandwich he had for lunch before going down to Washington Square. The three subway tokens. What else? He had three dollars and sixty-six cents that morning when he left the Bronx. He knows because he counted his money on his way downtown, on the subway. He's still missing thirty-five cents. He calculates again. Oh yes, of course, *The New York Times* for the ads. And the pack of cigarettes. He takes out his pack of Gauloises and lights one. Dammit, it's almost empty. He cannot remember what else he spent his money on. He replays the entire day in his mind. He feels his bones crack and he shivers. Sucette's smiling face appears in a remote corner of his confused mind.

He is hungry and thirsty too. He walks over to the drinking fountain at one end of the waiting room, keeping an eye on his suitcase back at the bench. Takes a long gulp of water. It's cold. Then he goes to the candy machine. He hesitates in front of it, holding his nickel with two fingers. Should he get one of those little packages of cookies? Three cookies in one package with peanut butter in between. It might be more nourishing than a candy bar. But he doesn't really like peanut butter. He finally decides on an almond Hershey.

He waits until he's back on his bench to eat the candy. Then he smokes another cigarette. There are four left now in the pack. Tomorrow he'll buy a newspaper and look through the help wanted ads. If he gets in line early enough maybe he'll be lucky. He wonders what to do with his suitcase when he goes looking for a job. He can't keep lugging it around. But he doesn't want to lose it either. Everything he owns is in that suitcase, even the old photographs of his parents and two sisters who died during the war. It'll look stupid to go apply for a job with a suitcase. He may have to leave it in one of the lockers at the station, even if it means wasting another nickel.

He sits for a while longer contemplating his problems. How long can he go on living in a world that systematically disenchants? If only someone had warned him against the inauthenticity of the American dream. If only he had spoken to her. It would have been so easy. And again Sucette's face appears in his head. He leans over and touches her eyes. Now she is standing naked in the alcove of her apartment, and Moinous puts his arms around her. In the fervor of his embrace he whispers to her, Love is the rift that rises above all things. He must have heard this somewhere. Sucette moves away from him and says, Though true love stories teach how to talk of love, they do not teach how to make love, and her face fades away. Moinous's eyes have closed involuntarily and he almost slides off the bench.

He decides to try to get some sleep. He pushes his suitcase snugly on top of the bench, at one end. He'll use it as a pillow, and this way it'll be safe. Nobody will be able to steal it from him. He takes off his overcoat to cover himself. He lies on the bench, on his side, facing the back, his knees folded against his stomach. He's tired now, but cannot fall asleep. He listens to the old man wrapped in newspapers cough and snort, and to the old lady with the umbrella who continues to talk to herself. He hears the siren of a police car, or an ambulance, screech in the street. He must have been more tired than he thought because soon he drops off into sleep, eve.. though he thinks he is awake, and keeps telling himself, Go to sleep, go to sleep. Once again Sucette appears behind his closed eyes, but only as a blur. He cannot remember how she looks. He sees only her pale blue eyes, and the smile. He feels ashamed. Ashamed to be poor and to be in love at the same time.

Stretched on the hard bench in restless sleep, Moinous has two dreams. In the first one he is standing in the middle of a crowd of curious onlookers in front of which a series of executions is taking place, and this puzzles him. Everyone is wearing a colonial helmet with a chin strap, except him. The victims are being tortured and then decapitated. Suddenly one of the executioners and two helpers come toward him, for it is his turn now, he is told. This horrifies him terribly. He was not expecting this. But he does not resist. Instead, he smiles. In the dream he remembers that he has dreamed this dream before and he knows that the images will be erased when he awakens because that recurrent dream has the quality of not being remembered except within the dream itself. But then the executioner pulls him by the hair and drags him on the ground while the two helpers kick him in the back and in the groin. Moinous tries to scream, but no sound comes from his throat.

Moinous shivers in his sleep. Instinctively he wraps the overcoat tighter around himself. Sleep does not always bring relief to fear. In the second dream Moinous is sitting in a movie theater next to a woman. She whispers something to him and caresses him between the legs. He shudders. At the end of the movie they walk out together, arm in arm. They arrive in front of her apartment, in a street crowded with bordellos. She opens the door and leads him into her room. A blue room full of exotic objects, among them a stuffed pigeon. A black cat is sitting on the dresser, but Moinous cannot tell at first if it is a real cat or a ceramic statue. It doesn't move, though the eyes are staring at him. Moinous and the woman are about to make love when a thought comes to his mind. This woman is a prostitute and probably diseased. He rises quickly from the bed and looks between the woman's thighs. There is fire there. A yellow flame which almost burns his face as he looks down. He runs to the window which is open and jumps into the garden from the second floor. He feels a pain in his legs. In the garden he climbs, as a timorous woman does on an armchair at the sight of a mouse or a huge spider, to the top of one of the stone blocks framing the entrance gate. He remains standing on this pedestal like a statue. Just as he is about to jump off into the street, he realizes that, in fact, he is standing on the highest level of the Eiffel Tower, and checks himself. For a moment he considers climbing down the exterior of the tower using the steel beams, but knowing his mortal fear of heights, he changes his mind and resigns himself to waiting for the next elevator. Suddenly the platform becomes the crater of a dead volcano, then a ship deck, then the top flight of a lighthouse. It is raining hard, and a thick fog prevents him from seeing where he is. He no longer knows when he will be able to come down.

Moinous feels a tremendous pain in his left leg, but he is

not sure if that pain is in the dream or if it is real. The pain shoots up his leg again and he wakes up. He rubs his eyes with his hand, and then sees this policeman standing over him, hitting the sole of his shoe with his club. Moinous starts up. The policeman is talking to him. Hey buddy, wake up, wake up. Show me your ticket.

What ticket? Moinous doesn't understand.

Your ticket. You know. If you're gonna spend the night here you gotta have a train ticket.

Moinous still doesn't understand. A train ticket to where? He asks the cop.

The policeman notices Moinous's accent. Eh, you're a foreigner, huh?

Moinous motions yes with his head.

Well, lemme explain something to you, Mack. If you're gonna sleep in Grand Central Station, you gotta have a train ticket. You understand? I don't make the rules, the cop goes on. City Hall makes the rules. Otherwise this place would be full of bums, and there wouldn't be no room for the regular customers.

Moinous is beginning to understand. Yes, okay. I think I understand. A ticket. But I'm not going anywhere. I'm just. He doesn't know if he should explain his situation. Explain that he's been kicked out of his room, and all the rest.

Don't matter. You still need a ticket, the policeman explains while twirling his club. Look, you're a foreigner, so I'm not gonna make trouble for you. I'm gonna let you stay here tonight. Okay. Just tonight. But if you wanna sleep in Grand Central Station again tomorrow, you better buy a ticket.

To where? Moinous asks trying to sound as civil as possible.

Oh, anywhere. I don't give a damn. Just buy a ticket to 125th Street, that's good enough by me. You get it buddy? 125th Street. The cop gives Moinous another blow with his club on the sole of his shoe, but gently this time. Don't forget. Buy a ticket. And the policeman walks away shrugging his large shoulders.

Moinous sits on the bench, dumbfounded. He mumbles to himself, What a place. What a strange place this country is. A ticket just to sleep on a bench in a train station. Moinous shakes his head. This is not irony, he thinks, this is cringing cynicism. He looks up at the clock. Three twenty-five. Still too early to go out and look for a job. He lies down on the bench again, and wraps the overcoat around his body all the way up to his nose. He doubts he'll be able to fall asleep. What a day, what a day it has been, he murmurs as he folds his legs against his stomach.

While Moinous is lying on his bench in the waiting room of Grand Central Station, trying to catch a few more hours of sleep before resuming his struggle with life, Sucette in her apartment on 105th Street is working on her short story. She is wearing her white terry-cloth wraparound robe and a pair of matching mules. She has tied her blond hair into a ponytail. Sitting at her desk, a huge antique piece of furniture which used to belong to her great-grandfather, she is typing on her Smith-Corona. She's been writing since nine o'clock. Six pages already. It's going well.

Her creative writing instructor at Columbia, Daniel B. Dogson, is really going to like what she's doing now with this story. He told her it needed more emotion, and also an element of suspense. Wait till he reads this new version. More emotion? Maybe he meant more explicit sexual allusions. He's so nice. So sensitive. And such a fine writer, with stories published in *Esquire* and *The New Yorker*. How lucky for Sucette to be working with such a distinguished author. She's learned so much from him in the past few weeks.

Sucette pulls the sheet of paper out of the typewriter. She paces the room reflecting on what she has just written. Isn't it amazing how the unexpected comes into a story? She sinks into her favorite armchair. A well-used red leather chair with brass nailheads along the seams. It used to stand in her father's office in Boston. She reads aloud the new section of her story. She smiles as she reads, holding the pages in one hand while letting a cigarette burn casually between two fingers of the other hand. She crosses her legs and her thighs are exposed.

She has introduced a new character in the story. A young man Susan meets in the streets of New York City. Susan Wakefield is the protagonist of her story. A tall statuesque blonde of rare sensibility but stubborn determination. That's how Sucette describes her. Susan meets the young man on Washington Square while participating in a political demonstration. Sucette stops reading. Crushes her cigarette in the ashtray next to her. She wonders if this may not be too close to her own experience. Too autobiographical.

Oh well, if Dan Dogson thinks it's too obvious, too factual, she can always change the name of the place later. That's how it came out. Spontaneously. And Dan did say once, when discussing the creative process in fiction writing, that reality is often unconscious, and therefore it is not always possible to control how it inserts itself into fiction. Conscious elements, on the other hand, he added, are usually narrow and seldom used outright. Sucette was not sure what he meant then, but now she understands how it works in her story. Obviously the young man Susan meets by chance is modeled on the real person with whom Sucette exchanged smiles that afternoon, even though she did not speak to him. He simply lodged himself in her subconscious and now reappears in her story almost surreptitiously as a fictitious character. That makes sense. It is through him that the necessary emotional conflict will be created.

Sucette starts reading again. From the beginning of the story. Susan Wakefield comes from a good Anglo-Saxon family in Boston, but she runs away from home when she turns nineteen and comes to New York to confront real life. There she gets involved in radical politics. She even joins the Communist Party and becomes a member of a cell. For Susan this represents the ultimate gesture of revolt against her family and her puritanical background, especially during the period when the story takes place. The early fifties.

Three times a week, in the evening, Susan goes to meetings to discuss Marxist ideology and socialist strategy with the members of her cell. There are twenty of them, including Susan. They discuss various ways of indoctrinating the workers into the Party. Susan doesn't say much at these meetings, but she listens intently. She's told to get a job in a factory in Brooklyn. A lampshade factory. There she will gradually but carefully talk to the workers during coffee breaks, or after work, and explain to them how they are being exploited by Capitalism, and how the rich are getting richer while the poor are getting poorer.

Sucette has already written this part of the story. She is particularly pleased with the section where Susan becomes emotionally involved with a young black man who is one of the most outspoken members of her cell. In the story he's called Tommy Blake. Susan likes what he has to say. His angry fervor, and the passionate way he talks about human misery. She likes his deep, concerned voice. After all, Tommy knows what he's talking about. He grew up in the ghettos of Chicago where he suffered poverty and humiliation. But now he has found a way to fight back. As a member of the Communist Party he no longer feels he is being exploited, for not only has he gained dignity and a sense of purpose in life, but he has achieved fraternity with his fellowmen. Sucette likes the way she has written this passage.

Now she is reading the section where Paul Robeson, the black actor who used to be with the controversial group called the Provincetown Players, comes to Susan's cell to speak to them about a huge demonstration which is being planned by the Party and which will take place on Washington Square. In February or March. It will be a very important rally, and everyone must show up. We're going to denounce McCarthy and his cohorts once and for all. Sucette is not happy with the way she has phrased all that. Also she doesn't know where to insert the bit of information she once read about Paul Robeson when he refused to play the part of a Harlem black because he was primarily cast for his natural sense of rhythm. Sucette makes a note in the margin about asking Dan how to rewrite this section. She lights another cigarette, takes a deep puff, and then goes on reading.

Susan didn't know much about human misery before she joined this cell. But now she is very concerned, and very committed, even though she is still quite shy. Sucette stops reading and scribbles something above the word shy, *and unsure of herself*. What a daring move, Sucette thinks while biting the end of her pencil, to have Susan get emotionally involved with a black man. Eventually, in another part of the story, Susan sleeps with Tommy and imagines herself to be in love with him. They even talk about the possibility of getting married, but Sucette is not sure that it would be credible. Not only because Susan is much younger than Tommy, but because, after all, one doesn't just do that sort of thing. It would be the absolute gesture of rebellion against the narrow-mindedness and bigotry of America. This part of the story needs a lot more work. And more depth too. Maybe Daniel Dogson can make suggestions as to how it can be worked out in a credible fashion.

The pages Sucette is now reading to herself deal with the new character she has introduced in the story. The young man Susan meets on Washington Square during the demonstration. A pure chance encounter. They bump into each other.

Oh, excuse me, Susan says with a smile.

No no, it was my fault, the young man apologizes. And he too smiles.

It's raining hard and the young man is soaking wet.

Why don't you come under my umbrella, Susan suggests
with a fraternal smile. You're going to catch a cold. They
stand close to each other. Someone on a platform is making a speech. Bellowing raucously through a megaphone.
Something about the Party, brothers, Marx, capital, daily
bread, the Huacos, fraternity, love.

What's happening here? The young man asks Susan.

Oh. You mean. You're not? Susan hesitates. It's a politi-
cal rally against our corrupted capitalistic government.
We are denouncing HUAC. You know, the House Un-
American Activities Committee.

Oh. The young man shakes his head as if he understands what Susan is talking about. He moves closer to her
because the rain is dripping off the umbrella on his shoulder. They smile at each other connivingly.

At first Sucette made the young man an Italian. Called
him Marco. She thought it would be more interesting for
the story if the young man was to be a foreigner. But then
she changed that. She really doesn't like Italian men. She
finds them too aggressive and too greasy. She decides to
make him French. Yes, Frenchmen are more subtle in
their ways, more suave. And this way Sucette can use
some of the French expressions she knows. Of course,
she'll have to check her French dictionary to make sure of
the spelling. Dan Dogson says that it's all right to use some
foreign expressions in a story for local color as long as one
does not abuse them. In the first draft Sucette calls the
young man Maurice, because two summers ago, when she
spent her vacation in France, she met someone by that
name. A fascinating person. He was an artist. A sculptor.
Un anarchiste famélique, is how he defined himself. Su-

cette was fond of him, and for a few weeks they had a good time together, discussing art and politics. They even took a trip together down through the Dordogne region to visit the Lascaux caves because Maurice wanted to see the prehistoric drawings. Two marvelous weeks, even though Sucette had to pay all the expenses. She sat for him in the nude, and he made a beautiful full-length statue of her. She never had such an exciting vacation, but when she announced that she was going back to America, Maurice got angry and the relationship disintegrated. Oh well, he was not right for her anyway, she reflected later. Finally Sucette changes the name again in her story. Instead of Maurice she invents a name for the young man Susan meets on Washington Square. A totally made-up name.

Sucette smiles as she reads the name aloud. Moinous. It's like a pun, though it does sound like a real name, a real French name. The other students in the class will probably not get it, but Dan will. He knows French. Moi and Nous. And besides, Susan sort of explains in the story why she gives this nickname to the young man when they become intimate. I call you Moinous, she tells him, to have a sense of togetherness with you.

Sucette doesn't know yet what will happen between Moinous and Susan, but she's pleased with the new twist in her story. It has lots of possibilities. Except that it's not going to be easy to write because she has to invent everything. Perhaps Susan will take Moinous to one of the meetings of her cell. By then, of course, they will be lovers, and there will be a crisis because Tommy is jealous and he starts an argument with Susan. Isn't that what Dan Dogson wants? More conflicting situations. Sucette has not yet written this part of the story, but she is all excited in anticipation of the work ahead.

She likes her creative writing class. All week long she looks forward to it. To those Thursday evenings when the class meets. It's a good group of young writers. Some of them quite talented, though none has yet published anything. But Daniel Dogson says that to become a writer requires a lot of patience and determination. He's such a superb teacher. This class has been a salvation for Sucette, especially since, lately, she's been feeling lonely and somewhat miserable with her own state of mind.

Sucette is already considering taking a poetry workshop in the fall. She prefers fiction, but she also writes poems occasionally, and she understands that the poetry class is very interesting.

In fact, one day, later, when Sucette & Moinous have been together for several months, she tells him that he should come and sit in on her poetry class. Just once. You'll see how interesting it is. And who knows, you too may start writing poetry. The teacher, Leonie Adams, is such a marvelous poetess. You should hear her read poetry. It's an experience. So one evening Moinous goes with Sucette to her poetry class at Columbia University. This is much later. In October. Or perhaps November.

A young pretty brunette, perhaps a bit too skinny for Moinous's taste, is reading her new poem to the class. It's a long piece, and somewhat obscure for Moinous. At one point during the reading he leans over and whispers to Sucette, Who is this guy Eddypuce she keeps mentioning?

A look of astonishment appears on Sucette's face, but all she can say is, Shhh, I'll tell you later after class. Pay attention now. And so Moinous concentrates, even though he doesn't really understand the poem.

After the brunette has finished reading her poem there is a long and lively discussion, and everyone agrees that it's a very good poem but that it needs more work. Especially in the final two stanzas. Then Leonie Adams says something about poetic ambiguity, and the class is dismissed. As Moinous & Sucette walk out of the room, he tells her again, I still don't know who this Eddypuce guy is.

Sucette cannot believe Moinous is that ignorant, and that he has never heard of Oedipus. In her usual kind way she tells him that Oedipus is a mythological figure. It's the story of a young man who accidentally kills his father and then marries his mother. He doesn't know this of course, and when later he discovers what he has done he puts out his eyes. It's a very moving and beautiful story which has a great deal of symbolic meaning.

I think it's a gory story, Moinous says. I don't understand why people want to write poems about this guy.

Later that evening, back in Sucette's apartment where Moinous has been living since the day when finally forty-two days of senseless hesitancy were wiped out in a few minutes of passion and the two lovers floated into easy oblivion, they go on discussing Oedipus. Sucette takes down her copy of *Bulfinch's Mythology* from her bookshelves and reads to Moinous the whole passage where the story of Oedipus is recounted.

Laius, king of Thebes, was warned by an oracle that there was danger to his throne and life if his newborn son should be suffered to grow up. He therefore committed the child to the care of a herdsman with orders to destroy him; but the herdsman, moved with pity, yet not daring entirely to disobey, tied up the child by the feet and left him hanging to the branch of a tree. In this condition the infant was found by a peasant, who carried him to his master and mistress, by whom he was adopted and called Oedipus, or Swollenfoot.

Many years afterward, Laius on his way to Delphi, accompanied only by one attendant, met in a narrow road a young man also driving a chariot. On his refusal to leave the way at their command, the attendant killed one of his horses, and the stranger, filled with rage, slew both Laius and his attendant. The young man was Oedipus, who thus unknowingly became the slayer of his own father.

Shortly after this event the city of Thebes was afflicted with a monster which infested the highroad. It was called the Sphinx. It had the body of a lion and the upper part of a woman. It lay crouched on top of a rock, and arrested all travelers who came that way, proposing to them a riddle, with the condition that those who could solve it should pass safe, but those who failed should be killed. Not one had yet succeeded in solving it, and all had been slain. Oedipus was not daunted by these alarming accounts, but boldly advanced to the trial. The Sphinx asked him, What animal is that which in the morning goes on four feet, at noon on two, and in the evening upon three? Oedipus replied, Man, who in childhood creeps on hands and knees, in manhood walks erect, and in old age with the aid of a staff. The Sphinx was so mortified at the solving of her riddle that she cast herself down from the rock and perished.

The gratitude of the people for their deliverance was so great that they made Oedipus their king, giving him in marriage their queen, Jocasta. Oedipus, ignorant of his parentage, had already become the slayer of his father; in marrying the queen he became the husband of his mother. These horrors remained undiscovered, till at length Thebes was afflicted with famine and pestilence, and the oracle being consulted, the double crime of Oedipus came to light. Jocasta put an end to her life, and Oedipus, seized with madness, tore out his eys and wandered away from Thebes, dreaded and abandoned by all except his daughters, who faithfully adhered to him, till after a tedious period of miserable wandering he found the termination of his wretched life.

Wow, what a fantastic story. Moinous is all excited by what he has just heard. What kind of a book is this? He takes the book from Sucette and looks at it. I'm going to buy a copy of this *Bulfinch's Mythology* and read the whole thing from beginning to end. This is the greatest story I've every heard.

There is a moment of silence between them while they both smoke a cigarette. Then Sucette explains to Moinous Freud's interpretation of this ancient myth, and how the Oedipus complex has transformed our understanding of human relations. Especially our relationship with our parents.

Moinous is fascinated. But then he says to Sucette, Let me ask you something. Since I had never heard of this guy Oedipus until today, does that mean that I have lived all my life, I mean the twenty-three years of my life, without any of that complex? After all, since I am an orphan, I mean since I lost my parents during the war when I was still very young, I really never had a chance to want to kill my father and sleep with my mother. At least not that I can remember. I suppose that makes me somewhat of a special case. Don't you think?

Well, no, because you see it's not that simple, Sucette replies, but does not elaborate. Shall I fix us some coffee? she asks as she gets up from her chair.

Yes, that would be nice, Moinous answers. And then let's go on with our discussion.

While fixing the coffee in the kitchen, Sucette wonders if indeed in Moinous's case much of his difficulties with life, and particularly with social situations, may not have something to do with his ignorance of the Oedipus myth. A few moments later, as the two of them sit at the table sipping their coffee, Sucette says, No it's not that simple. Because, you see darling, only in appearance is the Oedipus complex a beginning, either as a historical origin or as a structural foundation. In reality it is a completely ideological state which can occur any time in the life of an individual. And this applies to everybody.

You lost me. I don't understand what you're talking about. It's all Greek to me.

Let me try to explain it differently. The Oedipus complex is always and solely an aggregate of destination fabricated to meet the requirements of an aggregate of departure constituted by a social situation. Therefore, it can be applied to anyone anytime in spite of one's social or historical origin.

Does that mean that one can never escape that Oedipus complex? Moinous sounds disappointed as he says this.

Well, it depends. Sucette smiles. Oh, it's not that terrible. You see, Freud explains somewhere that from the time of puberty onward, the human individual must devote himself to the great task of freeing himself from his parents, and only after this detachment is accomplished can he cease to be a child and become a mature member of the social community. Of course, a lot of people never manage to do that, never succeed in breaking away from their parents. In a way, you and I are fortunate. Me because I did it deliberately and willfully, and you because of your unfortunate childhood.

Okay, I understand, but in my case don't you think it's a reverse process? If you think of it carefully, as an orphan I seem to be constantly looking for a mother and even a father in all my emotional involvements. Even with you. Now don't get me wrong. I'm not saying this because you're older than me. I'm only speaking in general. But it's true, it seems that I always get involved with older women. I mean older than me. But still, that's not the point. If I were to accept what you are saying, or what that guy Freud says, then for me, as a displaced person, there would be no hope of ever being able to achieve maturity.

Sucette suddenly looks annoyed. You never take anything I say seriously, she says getting up from the table to clear the cups away.

To which Moinous replies with a little sarcastic grin on his face, as if inventing the phrase on the spot, Seriousness is a quality for those who have no other qualities.

Obviously Moinous's sordid experiences of life have not equipped him for the confounded affairs of humanity, especially not psychological affairs. By the time this conversation takes place, the relationship of Moinous & Sucette has reached such a degree of tenseness and mutual suspicion that they hardly ever agree on anything. Their love is moving quickly toward its inevitable disappointment.

Nevertheless, had Sucette known Moinous at the time she writes her story about Susan Wakefield, she would certainly have incorporated this amazing conversation about Oedipus into the story. Perhaps she will use it later, in some other story, after Moinous has departed.

At this moment, however, still sitting in her dark red leather chair, holding the pages of her story in her hand, Sucette wonders what she will do with the new character she has invented. How can she use him to make Susan's story more interesting? More emotional?

It's too late tonight to work on this. Sucette gets up from the chair, puts her papers neatly into a folder, turns off the light above the desk, and walks to the alcove where the bed is located. She unwraps her robe and drops it to the floor. Steps out of her slippers. For a moment she stands naked next to the bed. She stretches her arms above her head and yawns. The white cheeks of her behind pinch together involuntarily. She's tired now. She gets into bed. What a day, what an incredible day it has been. Just as she's about to fall asleep Moinous's gentle face appears before her eyes. Sucette smiles.

THREE

Sucette awakens. She lazily un-
folds her arms and legs from a rest-
ful night of sleep and lies flat on her
back. She stretches. Yawns. Pushes the blankets
off her body with her feet. Passes her hand slowly
across her stomach and up over her breasts. She always
sleeps in the nude. Even during the winter. Her apartment
is well heated. It's going to be a nice day. She feels it.

She worked on her short story late into the night. The
story of Susan Wakefield. It's almost finished, except for
the final scene and a few minor revisions. It's been two
weeks since she introduced the new character. Two
weeks, in other words, since Sucette & Moinous smiled at
each other on Washington Square. It was not easy to get
him into the plot. But now she's pleased with the way the
story is going. And Daniel Dogson really likes the new version. Especially the new character she invented. Moinous!
Hey that's good, very good, he says with an approving nod
toward Sucette when she reads the new version to the
class. Very nicely done. It adds an interesting dimension
to the dramatic development of the narrative. Sucette
reaches for her cigarettes on the nightstand, takes one out
but does not light it. She is pensive. The ending of the
story still troubles her.

Sucette looks at the alarm clock on her nightstand. Oh
wow, eleven already. She'd promised herself to get up
early. So much to do. It's going to be a fantastic day. She
knows it. She'll have breakfast out. Yes, that will be nice.
Well, it'll be lunch really at this time. Besides, her refriger-

ator is empty. Sucette has been so busy working on her story these past few days, she has not even had time to go marketing. She's grown very fond of her new character. She thinks about him all the time. Even now, while taking her shower. It's become an obsession, as if he were real. Yes, it's like being involved in a real love affair.

She'll have lunch near Fifth Avenue. Perhaps at Schrafft's, she decides while getting dressed. She must stop at Lord & Taylor's to pick up her new coat. Today is Thursday, and they promised to have it ready on Thursday. Then maybe she can catch a movie. There is a new Kurosawa playing in the Village she's been wanting to see. Sucette loves Japanese films. But before that she'll go to the French bookstore in Rockefeller Center, it's only a short walk up from Lord & Taylor's, to buy Simone de Beauvoir's new novel. *Les Mandarins.* It's supposed to be very good. That's what Richard says. It'll be nice to read a book in French for a change. And maybe it'll give her some ideas for her story since Moinous is a Frenchman. It's going to be a wonderful day. Even though it looks like rain.

Meanwhile Moinous is washing dishes. He's been at it since six that morning. Yes, he finally gets a job, as a dishwasher in a cafeteria on Sixth Avenue, corner of 44th Street. Right next door to Honest Abe's Pawn Shop where he hocks his raglan tweed coat when he reaches the end of his money, soon after he is evicted from his furnished room in the Bronx and forced to sleep on a bench in the waiting room of Grand Central. They give him two dollars for his coat. But that'll keep him going for a couple of days, especially since he got the job in the cafeteria. He's been washing dishes for two weeks now. Well, nearly two weeks.

When Moinous wakes up in the waiting room of Grand Central, two weeks earlier, around five in the morning, his body aching from the hard bench, he leaves his suitcase in a locker, buys a newspaper, circles the possible jobs in the Want Ads while drinking a cup of coffee and chewing on a piece of toast at Freddy's on Broadway, and by five-thirty he stands in the job line. But again no luck that day.

Like thousands, millions of other desperate and jobless Americans, Moinous once more realizes that hope is merely the false expression one gives to it. But then there is an economic recession, he's told repeatedly, and things are not getting better in this great land of opportunity. Yet, without going so far as to say that Moinous sees the world darkly, that would be too easy, it is certain that he sees it in a way inordinately confused. In fact, in his search for a measure of prosperity, he often misjudges the distance separating him from a potential job, and often stretches out his hand for what is far beyond his reach. This has also been the case in his emotional relations with others, especially with women. Whatever he seeks is usually unattainable. What bothers Moinous the most, however, as he vainly continues to try to understand America, is the fact that Capitalism produces not only wealth for certain people, but also happy people whose worldly enterprise complements and completes the work of the system. That some people begin and end with less than others must be part of that scheme. At least, that's what Moinous thinks as he goes from one job line to another. Usually in the rain.

By midafternoon he is again aimlessly wandering the

streets of New York. He doesn't want to spend another night in that waiting room. First because the policeman may show up again, and second because he doesn't want to waste the money for a train ticket, not even to 125th Street. That would be stupid.

Around nine that evening he does go back to the station to pick up his suitcase. It may not be safe to leave it in the locker overnight. Then he walks down 42nd Street to Times Square. The movies are going full blast. And lots of people are standing around in the street. The neon signs and the marquees flashing their indecent lights into the rainy night.

One of the movie theaters has a special rate. Only thirty-five cents for three features. Open all night. Moinous counts his money without taking it out. He feels the coins inside his pocket with his fingers as he stands in front of the movie house. Fifty-seven cents. That's what he's got left now after the locker, the coffee and toast, the pack of Gauloises, but that's essential, without cigarettes he would go crazy, the newspaper for the ads, what a waste, day after day for nothing, and the noodle soup with crackers, custard pie, and coffee he had around four o'clock when he couldn't take it any more without food.

Thirty-five cents for a damn movie. Moinous decides to skip the hot dog he planned to have for dinner and buys a ticket for the cinema instead. At least here he may be able to stay the whole night, and even get some sleep if it's not too crowded and too noisy in the place. He feels a little embarrassed to go in with his suitcase.

The theater is packed. Mostly men. And smoky as hell. This is the period in America when smoking is still permitted in movie theaters. At least there is that bit of freedom left. The first picture has already started. Some Indians on horseback are screaming in the Far West while chasing a bunch of cowboys. Moinous is annoyed because he hates to miss the beginning of a film. Takes him a while to catch on to the story. He finds a seat in the rear and struggles to squeeze his suitcase underneath. Somebody in front of him turns around and says, Hey keep the fucking noise down, will you. Somebody else shouts in the dark, Yeah, what the fuck do you think this is, the Warldorf-Astoria? Moinous mumbles a vague apology to the people around him and sits down. But he keeps his feet on top of his suitcase. Just in case he dozes off. One never knows in a place like this.

Later, at the end of the third film, when he has to take a piss, he carries the suitcase along to the men's room. There is a funny smell of cooked cauliflower in the urinal, and Moinous feels sick to his stomach. He washes his face with cold water. He feels tired. And hungry too. He stares at his face in the mirror above the sink. He hasn't been able to shave in three days. He looks gray and haggard. His eyes are all puffy and his skin sallow.

On his way back to his seat he buys a chocolate bar at the candy counter. A Baby Ruth for five cents. That leaves him with exactly seventeen cents. The girl behind the counter gives him a sleepy but friendly smile. She looks a lot like the girl who bumped into him yesterday on Washington Square. Same blond hair, same pale-blue eyes, but of course it's not her. This one is younger, and not as tall, though just as beautiful. Moinous feels a strange pain in the left side of his chest. Just above the heart. He breathes hard two or three times. He hasn't thought about Sucette all day. Too involved with himself trying to find a way out of his miserable situation. But now his bones are hurting. Must be because of the hard bench on which he slept last night. Yes, must be because of that. Moinous is not very experienced in the pangs of love. Indeed, he has a splendid lack of common sense about love. He doesn't realize that his bones are hurting emotionally. He takes a look at the clock in the lobby. Twenty past two. Oh well, he'll watch the movies again. Perhaps he'll fall asleep in the middle.

The first two pictures are westerns. Moinous likes westerns. He likes adventure movies. He doesn't mind seeing these again. Besides, that's how he learned all about America when he was still in France. Yes, that's how he first discovered America, by watching cowboy and Indian movies dubbed into French, and also gangster films. His favorite actors are John Wayne and Edward G. Robinson. Moinous was very disappointed when he arrived in America and found that there were no more real cowboys, and all the gangsters had either been killed or thrown into jail. The third picture is a war movie in the Pacific. The American troops are trying to land on an island occupied by the Japanese. It's in black and white. Moinous thinks he's seen this one before. Doesn't matter though, because by the time it's shown again Moinous will be asleep.

Just as the Apaches are attacking the fort in the second western, and a lot of Indians and cowboys are dying all over the place, Moinous dozes off. His feet still on top of his suitcase. He doesn't really dream, but in his restless sleep he keeps thinking about the girl who smiled at him on Washington Square. Sucette, that is, even though he doesn't know her name. He even sees her dressed like an Indian squaw. She's beautiful. She has a black feather in her hair. Except that her blond hair makes it obvious that she's not a real Indian girl. She's in trouble. Her hands and feet are tied to a post with a rope, and there are flames all around her. Wild Indian warriors are dancing and screaming to the beat of a drum. Moinous would like to rush to her rescue, but he feels helpless. He has lost his cowboy hat, and when he reaches for his gun the holster is empty. Suddenly he jumps in his seat. Someone is touching his genitals. He straightens up. The movie theater is almost empty now, but there is a man sitting next to Moinous who smiles at him. A smile full of teeth. Moinous quickly moves his legs away.

You look like you're really tired, my friend, the man whispers. In the semi-darkness Moinous notices his curly hair and his thin mustache, and the leather jacket he's wearing. The man looks a bit older than Moinous. Late twenties or early thirties. Moinous is not very good at guessing other people's ages.

Just got into town? The curly man asks, still stroking Moinous's fly without the least reservation, even though Moinous has now crossed his legs. Ah, it's a rough life, I know. You don't have to tell me. Yeah, I know how it is to be all alone, the man coos. Moinous doesn't know what to do. He pretends to be watching the movie. The war picture is on again. The American Marines have recaptured the island, but there are lots of casualties, and the Japs are about to launch a counter-attack. The situation is critical.

The man leans closer to Moinous and now with his

other hand fingers his zipper while telling him all about the loneliness of life and the sadness of his little furnished room which, by the way, is just a couple of blocks from here and the place has two beds, and if you like you can come up and rest for a while. I know how it is. I've been on the road myself a number of times, and I'm always glad when somebody offers me a place to stay. We can listen to my records. I've got a good collection. You like music, don't you? And we can smoke some of the Turkish cigarettes a good friend of mine, a real doll, brought me as a present when he got back from the Middle East. They're divine. You smoke don't you? And the curly man goes on talking in a nervous squeaky voice while Moinous tries to extricate his suitcase from under the seat with his feet in order to get the hell out of there.

You know, it's okay with me if you spend the rest of the night at my place, the fellow goes on. I really don't care. On the contrary, you're welcome to stay as long as you want. I'm not selfish. My friends will tell you that. I like to share my things with others, especially when they're in trouble. I understand how it is sometimes in life. But if you want to rest for only a couple of hours because you really look exhausted from all your traveling, that's fine with me too. I won't bother you. Just an hour or two, the man insists while passing a finger on his mustache in a sensuous manner. Then he puts one hand on Moinous's shoulder while letting his other hand slide again toward Moinous's fly which, involuntarily, starts to bulge in a rather conspicuous fashion.

Moinous doesn't know what to say. How to react. Whether he should ignore the guy or punch him in the mouth. He's never experienced anything like this before. Not that he is naive about such things, after all he read some of Jean Genet's novels before he left France. Everybody was reading that stuff at the time. But the occasion never presented itself. Except once, in the latrine, when he was in the army, during basic training, in North Carolina, and someone in his barrack, a new recruit, asked him if he wanted a blow job. Moinous thought the guy was only kidding, and besides, at the time, he was not really sure what the expression meant. He was still struggling with his English when he got drafted into the army.

Suddenly Moinous shoves the curly man aside and stands up. *Fous-moi le camp, sale pédé*, he shouts, not realizing he's speaking in French. *Si tu continues à m'emmerder comme ça, je te mets mon poing dans la gueule et mon pied au cul.*

Somebody across the aisle from them shouts, Will you two fags shut the fuck up.

Oh, tu parles français, the man says with an atrocious accent. *Ah ça alors, j'y crois pas. Moi aussi, tu vois, parce que j'ai vécu à Paris pendant deux ans avec un gentil monsieur français que j'ai rencontré ici à New York. Ah, si c'est pas formidable qu'on se rencontre comme ça dans un cinéma. Quelle merveilleuse coincidence. Moi tu comprends, j'adore les français. Oui, j'adore tout ce qui est français. Allez viens. Viens chez moi, mon petit coco. On s'amusera bien, tu verras. Je te ferai des cochonneries.*

Moinous is furious now. Steaming. In spite of the fact that the man speaks French, which is quite a coincidence. Under normal circumstances he could exploit the situation and become friendly with this fellow and even accept his offer of a free bed for a couple of days. But instead, Moinous pushes the curly guy away with both hands. Leave me alone, dammit. I'm not interested in your room, and I don't give a shit about your records and your lousy Turkish cigarettes. So you speak French, big deal. *Comme une vache espagnole*. Get away from me. I've got enough problems without getting involved with a sneaky queer like you.

Okay, okay, don't get excited, the man says. I was just trying to be helpful. And he moves to another seat across the aisle from Moinous, but keeps glancing in his direction to see if he has changed his mind. Moinous picks up his suitcase and walks toward the exit. The pederast gives him the finger as he goes by.

Well, fuck you too, Moinous sneers as he holds up his fist in an obscene gesture.

Oh, I'd love it, I'd love it. In the ass especially, the queer replies with his smile full of teeth.

Moinous stands for a while in the deserted lobby of the theater. It's pouring outside. The candy counter is closed now. Too bad. He could have talked to the cute blonde who sold him the chocolate bar. And who knows. Anything. Anybody to soothe the pain of his loneliness. He presses his forehead against the glass of the entrance door and stares at the reflection of the cinema's marquee on the wet pavement. It's still dark in the street. With one finger Moinous draws the word *merde* on the steamy glass. He turns around to glance at the clock. Five-fifteen. Ah what an endless night.

For a moment Moinous considers walking to Grand

Central to leave his suitcase in a locker again. He can't keep lugging the fucking thing around. But that'd be another wasted nickel for a lousy locker. He finally steps out into the rain and walks up 42nd Street. He turns into the Avenue of the Americas. He smiles piteously as he looks up at the street sign and wipes the rain off his face with his sleeve.

Fuck fuck fuck this stinking country. The words spill out of his mouth almost in spite of himself. A reflex. It took Moinous some time to be able to utter the word *fuck* without any self-consciousness when he first came to America. In fact, it was not until he had been in the army for a couple of months, in jump school, that the word came out of him without his being conscious of it. That day, when the word *fuck* flew out of his mouth to qualify his feelings about army life, Moinous realized that he had suddenly begun to become an American, and he felt sad and nostalgic as a result, even though all his army buddies congratulated him for having made this monumental linguistic leap. And now, as he stops a moment on Sixth Avenue to switch his suitcase from his right hand to his left, the same sadness and nostalgia comes over him.

The cafeteria at the corner of 44th Street is open. Moinous goes in. The place is empty except for two decrepit old men who are discussing politics at one of the tables. The type of old men who never sleep. They are shouting at each other with cracked voices. A dark-haired young man in a dirty apron is sweeping the floor while whistling a tune. Behind the counter where the food is displayed, a fat bald man with an ugly crooked nose asks Moinous what he wants. The man looks imposing. Must be the owner of the place. One of his elbows is resting on top of the cash register.

A cup of coffee, please, Moinous says while staring at the macaroni and cheese which is bubbling in a large stainless steel pot under a yellow heat lamp.

You want cream and sugar?

No black, with just a little sugar, please.

Looks like you had a rough night, buddy, the fat bald man says to Moinous. Just got into town? He points to the suitcase. Where from? The West Coast?

Uh. Yeah. I mean, uh. Moinous stutters.

Here, that coffee'll warm you up. It's really coming down out there, wow. Can't make up its mind if it wants to shit or piss. You want a doughnut with the coffee? They're fresh.

How much for the doughnut? Moinous asks while trying to remember how much money he has left in his pants pocket.

Just a nickel. They're really fresh. Just came in a while ago.

And for the coffee?

What d'you mean? A nickel. Where you've been, fella? Coffee is always a nickel. Thank God for that.

Moinous hesitates. No, I'll just have the coffee.

The fat man hands him a cup on a saucer while shaking his head. Is it that bad? Here, have the doughnut, it's on me. Go ahead, take it. Take it, and don't tell me your problems. I've got my own. These are bad times, friend. Real bad times. And it's gonna get worse, believe me. Much worse, with the kind of crooked government we've got.

Taxes, and taxes and more taxes. I tell you, I wouldn't be surprised if before long I'm forced to close this joint.

Moinous doesn't answer. He simply nods approvingly and then walks away from the counter carrying his suitcase in one hand and the cup of coffee and doughnut in the other when the fat guy calls him back. Hey, fella, come back here a moment. Moinous stops and turns around, almost spilling the coffee in the process.

The man steps out from behind his counter and helps Moinous to a table. He sits with him. His breath smells of onion. Tell me, are you looking for a job? I need somebody for the dishes. The bum who was doing them quit on me during the night. Can you believe that. The lazy good-for-nothing bastard dropped everything in the middle of the night and just walked out. I tell you, it's not easy to run a business. You gotta deal with all sorts of miserable bums and lousy foreigners who can't even speak the language. Ah lemme tell you, I've seen some real beauties in this place, you wouldn't believe. Anyway, if you want the job, it's yours. You look like a decent fella. I haven't put up a sign in the window yet, but when I do, well lemme tell you, I'll have forty guys out there standing in line. So what d'you say?

Moinous is speechless. First touch of luck and of humanity in weeks. He almost chokes on his doughnut as he says, Oh yes, yes of course, I want the job. I can start right away if you want me to. I'm ready. And he stands up to put out his hand to the fat man in a gesture of gratitude. And you know, he adds, I've got experience. I did lots of K.P. when I was in the army.

Well, that's good, very good, but first finish your coffee,

and then I'll get you going in the kitchen. I've got a huge pile of dirty dishes waiting there, and by six o'clock this place is gonna be jammed full. The fat man gets up to go back to his counter, hesitates, then asks Moinous, Hey kid, where you from? You got an accent.

From France, Moinous answers. But I've been in this country for almost five years.

Ah, you're a frog. Well, that's okay with me. I like frogs. In fact I understand they appreciate good food. You're perfect for this place, right? the fat man says with a twisted smile as he gives Moinous a solid but friendly pat on the shoulder. Well, I'll be damned, a Frenchman. Not too many of youse guys around. In fact, you know something, you're the first one I ever hired in the thirty years I've been in this goddamn business. And lemme tell you, I've seen all kinds in that kitchen of mine. Chicanos, polacks, gooks, krauts, schwartzes. I even had a Swede in there once. I'm not kidding. A huge hunk of a guy with eyes as big as blue Ping-Pong balls. And dumb. You wouldn't believe how dumb he was. He didn't last very long. I've never seen such a klutz. But you, you're the first Frenchman ever. Well, at least from what I hear about you frogs, you're not like the rest of those lazy foreigners we've got these days hanging around this city doing nothing. You know what I mean. You'll do good in this place. I can tell.

Oh yes, I'm sure, I will, Moinous replies while sipping his coffee.

The fat man gives his new dishwasher another friendly pat on the shoulder as he gets up to go back to his counter, and then asks, Hey tell me Frenchy, is it true what they say about youse frogs that you eat pussy? Moinous blushes while his new boss breaks out into obscene laughter. Back behind his counter, he shouts across the room, Oh, by the way, Frenchy, one more thing. Anything you break in the kitchen is automatically deducted from your pay. Right. You got that?

And so two days after he & Sucette smile at each other, therefore two days after he's evicted from his furnished room in the Bronx, Moinous gets a job, and even a place to sleep. Luck is perhaps flowing his way at last.

The other young man who works in the cafeteria, Joseph, a really nice fellow, about the same age as Moinous, of Armenian descent, tells Moinous about this place where he lives on 23rd Street, you know, between Second and Third. Yeah, they got rooms for rent there. Cheap too. Six bucks a week. Well, you know, nothing fancy. I mean, it's not the Hilton. Just a bed, a table, and a couple of chairs. You get the picture. No hot water. But what the hell, it's better than nothing. Bedbugs, yes. But you get used to them creepy things. I tell you, I was damn glad to find the place when I got into town from Detroit. You ever been there? I mean Detroit. What a shitcity man. Got laid off. Used to work at Chrysler, on the line, screwing bolts into the frame. What a fucking stupid job that was, the young Armenian explains while taking a cigarette break in the kitchen where Moinous is hard at work washing the plates and scrubbing the pots. The only problem is you gotta pay the fucking rent in advance for the whole week, otherwise no dice. Six bucks. I suppose you don't got that kind of dough. No, obviously not, else you wouldn't be working in this joint.

I have twelve cents left, Moinous says to his newfound friend, but maybe you could loan me the six dollars until payday. I'll give it back to you as soon as I get paid.

Me? You must be kidding. I got maybe a buck left, not even that, to finish the week. We get paid on Monday here. And what's today? Thursday? No way, man. Honest, I just can't let you have that kind of dough. I mean, I would even let you stay in my room until Monday, but you see there is only one bed, a very narrow one. And besides, I mean, I got a friend.

Moinous doesn't know what to do. It would be so great to have a room and be able to get a good night's sleep. In spite of the bedbugs. He slept with bedbugs before. So at the end of this first day on the job, Moinous asks his new boss if perhaps he could let him have six dollars. You see, it's to pay for a room in advance, he explains.

The boss tells him, Look, I'm a nice guy, and I like you. You did a fine job here today, you're a good worker, but I just can't give you six bucks like that. How do I know you'll be back tomorrow? You see what I mean? I can't take that kind of chance, otherwise I may be up shit's creek again.

Oh, I'll be back. I promise. I swear, Moinous says with a look of deep integrity in his eyes. I really mean it. I need this job. And I like working for you. You've been so decent with me. I really appreciate what you did for me. It's just that.

Look, Frenchy, best I can do is give you what you've earned so far. You get fifty cents an hour. These days, believe you me, it's not bad. Better than most places. You work from six in the morning till two in the afternoon. The early shift, in other words. This place never closes. I've got other guys doing the afternoon and the night shifts. That's four bucks a day, six days a week. Right? You're off on Tuesdays. How's that sound?

Sounds tremendous, Moinous replies. Desperate as he is, he is not about to argue the terms of his new job. One must be humble in the struggle for survival.

Also you get one meal a day on top of that, the fat man goes on explaining. Only one though. Either breakfast when you come in or lunch before you leave. But that's all. And lemme warn you, no stealing food. No eating behind my back, or else you're out. You got that? I'll keep an eye on you. I'm not running a Salvation Army joint here.

Moinous keeps shaking his head up and down in total agreement as the boss goes on explaining the conditions of the job.

Okay. Fifty cents an hour plus one meal a day. That's twenty-four bucks a week. You get paid on Mondays, like everybody else. Later maybe I'll switch you to the night shift. You get an extra buck for that. Ten to six. But first I gotta see how you work out, for a couple of weeks. Is it a deal? Take it or leave it, Frenchy. I can't do any better.

Oh, it's fine, fine with me, Moinous answers. It's exactly the kind of job I was looking for. And I don't mind working at night. I've done lots of night shifts.

Good. As for the six bucks, here is what I'm gonna do. But you gotta understand, I don't usually do that. It's an exception. I'm gonna give you today's pay. You've done eight hours, I'll give you four bucks. That's the best I can

do. But you better make damn sure you show up tomorrow morning, you hear. Don't make an ass out of me. I can
be a mean bastard.

Oh, I will, I will. And I really appreciate what you're doing for me, Moinous says with a great deal of emotion in
his voice. You're a nice man. You can count on me. You'll
see, I'm a very responsible person.

So, did he give you the six bucks? Joseph asks Moinous
as they leave the cafeteria together.

He only gave me four. Best he could do he said. What
am I going to do? You sure you can't let me have the extra
two dollars, Moinous asks again. Just until Monday.

Honest, man, I can't. I'm really broke. I had a heavy
week. I tell you, if it wasn't for the food I eat in this lousy
joint, I would really be in trouble. But look, I got an idea.
You see this place, and the Armenian fellow points to
Honest Abe's Pawn Shop, next door to the cafeteria. Why
don't you hock your overcoat? I'm sure you can get at least
three maybe four bucks for it. Looks in good shape to me. I
know the guy in there, I'll talk to him.

Pawn his overcoat? Moinous never thought of that. Why
not. One learns so many things in America. So many ways
to keep going and conquer existence. Okay, Moinous says.
What the hell. Another month or so and the weather will
start improving. But you got to do the talking, he tells his
new friend as he follows him inside the pawn shop.

It's the first time Moinous enters such a place, though
later, after he & Sucette have parted, and he has returned
to the aloneness of his miserable life and to a further state
of joblessness, he will often frequent such places.

Hi there, Mr. Shapiro, the Armenian fellow says, I

brought you a customer. Don't cheat him, he's a good friend of mine.

At first Mr. Shapiro wants to give Moinous only a dollar and a half for his raglan tweed coat. He shows him how the lining is torn, a couple of buttons are missing, and the thing needs a good cleaning. But Joseph, who is a shrewd bargainer and a regular customer, convinces Mr. Shapiro to go for two dollars.

And so Moinous now has a room. And since he had a good meal of macaroni and cheese at the cafeteria, he feels happy. In fact, he sleeps soundly that night, in spite of the bedbugs which can't wait for him to get into bed to attack. He tries to dream about Sucette, but the dream fizzles out. He cannot summon her face to his mind. Later into the night though, he awakes in the middle of a wet dream, and while he wipes himself with the sheet Sucette's generous face appears on the wall facing the bed. She smiles at him compassionately.

At six the next morning he's back at the cafeteria. But now that Moinous has a job and a place to sleep, he doesn't spend as much time worrying about his personal problems. While washing the dishes, or wandering around the city after work, he thinks about Sucette and listens to his bones crack. He wonders how he can get to meet her again, and this time, for sure, talk to her. He even goes so far as imagining that Sucette is also frantically searching for him. Give a man a good meal, like a dish of macaroni and cheese, a place to sleep, and immediately he rearranges the affairs of the world.

Usually, after work, Moinous goes down to Washington Square to speak to his friend Charlie, the one-legged pigeon, but also to see if by chance Sucette has returned to the place where they smiled at each other. He sits on the same bench and waits for hours, even if it rains. And lately, since he hocked his overcoat, it rains all the time.

As soon as Charlie sees Moinous sitting on the bench, he hops over. Moinous tosses a few pieces of bread on the ground, and while the bird pecks away, he tells him that life, after all, is not that bad, and that he too should not despair, even though he has only one leg. He tells him about his new job in the cafeteria, and about his little room on 23rd Street, and about his Armenian friend. No, life is not that bad. I'm sure things will work out for you too, Charlie, you'll see. Of course, Charlie cannot answer, but he keeps squeaking at Moinous and begging for more bread crumbs.

Finally, when the bird is satisfied, he flies away to join the other pigeons on top of the arch. For though Charlie has great difficulty walking on the ground on his one leg, he has no problem flying like the other pigeons. It is fortunate for him that he has two wings. After Charlie flies away, Moinous remains seated on the bench looking around to see if Sucette is there on the Square searching for him. But day after day he walks away disappointed.

Sometimes, as he sits there in the rain and the cold, holding the lapels of his jacket tight around his neck since he no longer owns an overcoat, he replays in his mind the events of the afternoon when he & Sucette smiled at each other.

There he is standing in the rain in the middle of the noisy crowd which has gathered on Washington Square when someone bumps into him from the rear. He turns around and finds himself face to face with this lovely blonde who gives him a warm smile, but without saying a word. Moinous smiles back, and is about to apologize for his clumsiness when a man standing on top of the roof of a car starts making a speech, shouting through a megaphone, and the charming blonde turns toward the speaker. Moinous notices the sign she is holding high above her head. As the crowd presses toward the man who is speaking, Sucette drifts away from Moinous. He tries to elbow his way closer to her to ask her what this is all about, but the people on the Square are getting more and more animated as they now shout slogans in unison. Moinous is separated from the blonde, though he can make out her sign above the heads of the people.

What's going on? he wonders. And why are all these policemen surrounding the Square? Some on foot, others on horseback. What are all these speeches about blacklists, jobs, the Huacos, Roy Cohn, McCarthy, freedom of speech? Moinous doesn't understand, but he finds himself carried along with the spirit of the crowd and of the moment, and when they all break out into a song whose tune Moinous does not recognize, he hums along anyway, wishing he knew the words of that song.

The charming blonde is quite far from him now, but Moinous still sees her sign waving among the other signs people are holding up in the air. Yes, it is her sign because when she bumped into him he noticed what was written on it. WE DEMAND FREEDOM OF SPEECH & FREEDOM OF POLITICAL ACTION. Not much of a sign. Just a broomstick with a piece of cardboard tied to it at one end, but nonetheless it seems impressive to Moinous.

While he struggles to get closer to Sucette, it occurs to him that there is something incongruous about this rather beautiful and elegant blonde in her middle thirties. Moinous is not very good at guessing other people's ages. Yes, she seems out of place in this crowd, holding her broomstick high in the air and shouting slogans with the rest of them, many of them looking more like older versions of Moinous himself. Working-class types. Or more likely a group of unemployed workers.

She's really too elegant for the scene. Too sophisticated. But of course appearances can be deceiving. Still, she does seem too well dressed in her beige camel's-hair coat and her brown leather boots. Moinous is not very experienced in the matter of expensive clothes, but since his people were all tailors he recognizes fine quality fabrics such as in her coat when she bumps into him. Also, her blond hair, tied with care into a bun in the back of her head, which makes her perhaps look older and sterner than she is, indicates a certain class. She's not overly slender, but not fat either. Just plump. Attractively plump. Almost European in stature, Moinous thinks. Pale-blue eyes that keep moving around and sparkling with candid mischievousness. At least that's how Moinous sees Sucette in his mind as he replays again and again the scene of that afternoon on Washington Square.

Later, when he gets to know Sucette more intimately, he realizes that he was wrong about the candid mischievousness of her eyes. What he usually sees there, when they lie close to each other, is a kind of elusive sadness. But then Moinous often misreads the messages other people's eyes send him.

As he tries to follow the charming blonde's sign, since now he cannot see her anymore in the crowd, suddenly there is a great commotion. The policemen around the Square are charging into the crowd to disperse it. There is shouting and shoving and clubbing left and right, and everyone is running in all directions.

Moinous doesn't know what to do. So he stands there, still trying to find the blonde with the broomstick when he feels a tremendous pain on the side of his face. Right at the temple. A huge policeman is standing in front of him, his club raised ready to strike Moinous again. Moinous covers his face with both hands. He wants to explain to the policeman that he is not involved, that he is not part of this crowd, that he was just passing by, but before he can utter a word the club comes down again and hits him on top of the head. As he staggers and feels his knees buckle under him, he hears the policeman grunt, Get the hell out of here you filthy red. Moinous still doesn't understand what is going on, and why he is being assaulted like this. The thought flashes in his mind that this is not really happening, that he is in a movie, one of those Hollywood movies, full of riots and violence, he used to love to watch when he was still in France. But the pain at the side of his face is real enough.

Were Moinous watching this scene from a distance, he would probably reflect on its violence and confusion, and perhaps even formulate, in his own foreign way, a critique of America. But this is not the time for such a reflection since he is himself an actor, however, accidental his presence may be, in this little drama. And besides, Moinous would undoubtedly reach the conclusion that an ultimate critique of American violence is not possible because of the absence of a theory of chaos.

While Moinous speculates about the reality of what is happening, and the huge policeman in front of him is ready to strike him again with his raised club, he notices that some of the people in the crowd are struggling with the police, fighting back as best they can with their signs or their fists, though most of them are running from the Square. Moinous does not wait for the club to come down again. He takes off, full speed, on his wobbly legs, toward Fifth Avenue, right under the opening of the Washington Arch.

Moinous is not angry. No, just dumbfounded. The whole thing happened so quickly. The side of his face feels like it's paralyzed. He is still running at full stride while holding his hand over his temple. He finally slows down when he reaches the corner of 14th Street. He's puffing like a water buffalo. He stops and leans against the wall of a building. He feels dizzy. And of course, he's totally drenched. No one seems to pay attention to him. He rubs the side of his face, and when he looks at his hand, he sees blood there mixed with the rain.

This is Moinous's first involvement in politics, however accidental it may have been. Up to now his political inclinations have been rather unconscious. But that blow on the side of his face seems to awaken him to the realities of political life. Those fucking bastards, he says aloud in the middle of the street as he clenches his fist in front of his face.

Had Moinous spoken to Sucette earlier on Washington Square, it wouldn't be surprising if the two of them would now be discussing with fervor and agitation the deplorable state of affairs in America, probably over a cup of coffee. And by their second cup, Moinous, now totally radicalized, would be ready to join Sucette's political movement. But instead, in the pathetic confusion of the moment he loses her.

And now, as he stands in the rain at the corner of 14th Street and Fifth Avenue to catch his breath and wipe the blood from his face, Moinous looks around to see if by chance the charming blonde also ran in this direction. Perhaps she's there, among the passers-by, looking for him. But all he sees around him are unconcerned people hunched under their umbrellas rushing about their business without even a compassionate glance in his direction. If she were to appear in the crowd, perhaps she would talk to him, perhaps even suggest a cup of coffee together. But Sucette is nowhere in sight.

It occurs to Moinous that there is no point standing there in the rain, waiting in vain, but instead that he better get back to his room in the Bronx and see what happened with his landlady. By now she may have thrown his stuff out into the corridor. She's been threatening to do so for the past few days because he hasn't paid the rent.

For more than a week after Moinous gets the dishwasher job in the cafeteria, every day, after work, he goes down to Washington Square, and as he sits on the same bench he replays that scene over and over again. He even goes beyond the reality of the facts. He imagines that he & Sucette spoke to each other, and when the demonstrators are dispersed by the police, the two of them run together up Fifth Avenue. They finally stop near 14th Street, drenched with rain, breathless but safe. As they lean against the wall of a building, they suddenly start giggling connivingly, but then Sucette notices the cut on Moinous's face. She takes out her handkerchief and gently wipes the blood which is running down his cheek.

Does it hurt? she asks with great concern in her voice. It's a mean cut. Maybe you should see a doctor.

No, it's nothing. Really. Doesn't hurt at all, Moinous replies courageously.

Sucette then suggests that they stop somewhere for a cup of coffee. It'll do us good. Schrafft's is only a few blocks away. They walk up the street and go into the coffee shop, still giggling happily. By the second cup of coffee Moinous has told Sucette almost everything about his life. Words flow out in a continuous stream, in spite of his accent, as if language had been stranded for years deep inside of him. Sucette listens intently. She's a good listener. While Moinous talks on and on about himself she reaches across the table and takes his hand.

By the time they leave Schrafft's, Sucette has hardly revealed anything about herself, but she knows all the details of Moinous's miserable life. How he lost his parents and sisters during the war, when he was a boy, how he then worked on a farm in southern France, and how he came to America, after the war, almost five years ago, because he didn't know what else to do, how he struggled for the first two years, not only with the language but with life itself, before he was drafted into the army and then shipped to Korea, to fight the war, where he was almost killed in a foxhole near Inchon, and after that they sent him to Tokyo, where it was not as bad, and then how he just got out of the army, only a few months ago, and things are not going very well right now, because of the economic situation in America, and it's so hard to find a decent job these days, and New York is such a tough and lonely place, and how he has no real friends, except for Charlie, the one-legged pigeon. Sucette smiles tenderly when she hears about Charlie. Moinous even tells her about the problems he's having with his landlady in the Bronx. But things will improve, he's sure of that.

Sucette listens with tenderness. She has never met anyone like him before. Poor soul, whose life seems to be a series of stumblings from one misfortune to another. He sounds so sincere and yet so innocent, so full of optimism in spite of all his troubles. She likes him immediately.

A sentence she has read recently in a D. H. Lawrence novel echoes in her mind. *I want to find you where you don't know your own existence, the you that your common self denies utterly.* Yes, she would like to care for him without any preconceived idea of what she would want in return for her love. And so she's the one who suggests that they see each other again. No, she's sorry, but she can't stay with him now. She has a dinner engagement. It would have been so nice to go on talking like this. She has to rush back to her apartment. She's really really sorry about that. I hope you understand.

She gives Moinous her telephone number, though she explains that for the next few days she'll be out of town. She has to go up to Boston to visit her family. But after she returns, next week, he can call her anytime. You will, won't you, for sure, she says as she hands him the slip of paper on which she has scribbled her phone number. Moinous explains that he doesn't have a telephone because he doesn't plan to stay much longer in his furnished room in the Bronx, otherwise he would give Sucette his number too. But he promises to call her soon.

In a way Moinous is glad that things are working out this way, and he doesn't have to spend the rest of the day with Sucette. After he insists on paying for the coffees, he realizes that he has hardly any money left. At most a couple of dollars, maybe less. He's not sure now, even though he counted his money earlier that day. Had Sucette agreed to spend the evening with him, he would really have been in trouble. No doubt she would have wanted to go back to her place to change into dry clothes. By taxi, of course, and Moinous would have had to insist on paying for that too. Then they would probably go for dinner somewhere. In a quiet French restaurant. Yes, that would be appropriate. Poor Moinous would be so embarrassed to have to tell Sucette he's broke. It's better this way for now. Better to postpone the rest of this first meeting.

As Moinous sits on his bench, in Washington Square, day after day, he continues imagining his relationship with Sucette. He adds new details, new twists to the situation. Embellishing the words and the gestures that are exchanged, even though these may not be very original. Love stories, real or imagined, are always full of clichés and ready-made fantasies. However, Moinous never goes so far as exploring the first intimate moment of this liaison. The coming together in the darkness of the suave loins. Not because he lacks imagination, but because he wants that moment to be perfect in its eventual reality. But then, after a week or so of these futile imaginings, Moinous gives up going to Washington Square since he is now convinced that Sucette will not return. Perhaps she has already forgotten him. Lovers are often forgetful.

Instead, after he leaves the cafeteria, around two o'clock, he wanders in other parts of the city. Usually up Fifth Avenue. He likes to walk up and down that fancy avenue to look at the shop windows and at the people in the street, especially the women who go shopping in the expensive stores. He admires their legs. Their long, elegant legs that keep going up and up under the skirts to where it's warm, warm and cozy, but where only the imagination can venture. This makes him sad, because he feels that perhaps for the rest of his life he will seek what can never be attained.

Sometimes he stops at the Librairie Française, in Rockefeller Center, to look at the books and read the magazines. It is probably there, since it is destined, that one afternoon, let's say two weeks after the mutual exchange of smiles, Moinous & Sucette will meet again.

It's another rainy day. Moinous is standing in a corner of the bookstore reading a page of a recent French mystery novel of the Série Noire, when someone bumps into him accidentally. He turns around, and there stands Sucette. He cannot believe it's her, and for a moment he is speechless. He even blushes as if caught doing something wrong. A little redness also appears on Sucette's cheeks. She hesitates. Smiles. A smile that freezes on her face like a question mark.

Oh, it's you, she finally exclaims, as if she had been expecting to meet Moinous again. You remember, we . . .

Yes yes, on Washington Square, when they had that demonstration and the police . . .

They both seem unable to finish what they want to say. Yet there is a tone of intimacy in their voices, like that of old friends who meet again by chance after years of separation.

This is—I can't believe it, Sucette cries out.

What? What do you mean? Moinous is groping for words. He has an eerie feeling, as if Sucette just stepped out of one of the books on the shelves.

I mean. Do you? No, what I mean, are you French, by chance? Sucette is all excited and cannot refrain from showing her excitement and her happiness. And yet she feels clumsy standing there holding her purse, her umbrella, her Lord & Taylor box with her new coat in it, and the copy of Simone de Beauvoir's new novel she has just bought. She wishes she could put all these things down somewhere and look natural.

Yes, I am. Moinous shakes his head in the affirmative as if the fact that Sucette has guessed he's French gives him an advantage. I was born in Paris.

Wow, this is really unbelievable. Sucette also shakes her head while biting her lower lip in a sign of utter astonishment. There is more hesitation on her part. And then in a calmer voice she says, Yes I thought I noticed a French accent.

Oh yes, I still speak with an accent. But I don't understand what's so incredible? You mean that we meet again? Moinous doesn't know what else to say, but he wants to keep the conversation going for fear that she might vanish unless words continue to hold them together. He cannot tell her that in his mind he knew all along they would meet again like this.

No. Well. I mean, yes. That we meet again, but also that
you are French. It's just amazing.

There is further hesitation, further groping for words,
and then Sucette, bluntly. Are you doing anything right
now?

Me? Hmm. I'm—I'm just looking at these books, Moinous stammers, still unsure of where all this will lead.

No, I mean are you free right now? I don't want to seem
too, how shall I say? I don't want to appear too aggressive,
but how would you like to have coffee with me or something so we can talk? It's just that I have to tell you something. Something amazing. There is a trace of uncertainty
on Sucette's face as she speaks these words, as if she suddenly realizes she may have gone too far with this stranger. After all, they never spoke before. And he looks so
much younger than she.

Coffee? Together? Oh sure. Yes yes of course. Moinous
cannot believe this is happening to him.

How about Schrafft's? Sucette suggests. It's only a block
or two down the street, and it's my favorite coffeehouse.

Moinous agrees. At this point if Sucette had proposed
marriage on the spot, or some unnatural sexual act, or
even a dual suicide, he would have agreed without the
least hesitation. He still can't believe that she's here with
him, and that they are talking to each other. Almost the
same words he has rehearsed over and over again in his
mind for the past two weeks.

There is a moment of fidgety silence while the waitress
serves them coffee and asks if that will be all. How about a
sandwich or a piece of cake with your coffee? Sucette proposes, already taking charge of their relationship. And in-

deed, in the months to come, Sucette will always be ahead
of Moinous, anticipating every lapse. He finds her there
already at every point where he falters, ready to help him
to his feet and show him that it doesn't matter.

No, just coffee. With sugar. Two spoons. Thank you.

There is more silence. Moinous takes out his pack of
cigarettes and lights one.

Oh, Gauloises, Sucette exclaims. I haven't seen any of
these in a long time.

Oh, you've been to France? Moinous inquires with just
the right amount of surprise in his voice.

Oh yes, several times. I love it there. France is such a
beautiful country. And the food is so marvelous. Love stories always begin with exclamations and banal statements.

Moinous offers Sucette a Gauloise. She says No, thank
you, they're too strong for me, and lights one of her own
cigarettes. A Pall Mall. Then Sucette starts talking. Fast,
nervously, but happily, as if the words needed to be re-
leased from some deep recess inside her body. Moinous
sits quietly. His fingers are playing with a book of matches
on the table as he listens. He is still amazed to be here.
Amazed that she is real. That she is talking to him. That he
is sitting with her, the charming blonde who haunted his
mind for the past two weeks. His bones feel weak.

He looks at his hand fidgeting with the ashtray on the table. He tries to avert Sucette's eyes, but every so often he
glances up at her animated face. She's beautiful. More beautiful even than he made her to be in his mind. In his mental
image, however, he had not visualized the light freckles on
her face. And also, she's a bit more chubby than he remembered. But her eyes are lively, and so blue, just as he kept

seeing them in his dreams. She has lovely hands too. Very white. Moinous almost reaches across the table to touch one of her hands. But suddenly he feels shabby and humble in his working clothes. His dishwasher outfit. He is not wearing his sport coat and his good pants today. Just an old sweater under a worn-out beige zipper jacket and a pair of wrinkled pants. As he sits there listening to Sucette talk, he gradually surrenders to the charms of a virile self-pity. Sucette appears so secure, so reassurringly solid and elegant.

This is really unbelievable, she is saying. You see, I've been writing this story and—

Oh, you're a writer, Moinous interrupts with a glare of admiration.

Well, I'm trying to be. I'm still a beginner. I've written only one or two stories. But I take it seriously, and maybe someday I will make it. Who knows. Anyway, I've been working on this story, and a few weeks ago. In fact, the very day you and I. You and I saw each other on Washington Square. You remember, when we bumped into each other? Well, when I got home that evening I introduced a new character in my story. A young man. And for some reason, don't ask me why, I decided to make him French.

You mean, like me. Moinous cannot believe such things happen in real life.

Well, yes. In a way you could say that I modeled him after you, even though I knew nothing of you. After all we only bumped into each other that day, and you smiled at me.

And you too, Moinous bursts in.

Yes. Sucette smiles again, then shakes her head. It was such a messy afternoon. Anyway, I still don't know why I made that new character a Frenchman. I suppose because I like French people. But you know something, it works well in my story.

Oh this is—this is unbelievable. You mean to say I'm in your story. I just can't believe it, you were thinking about me all that time while you were writing your story. Moinous is visibly thrilled and cannot hide his joy. His smiling gaze struggles to the extreme limits of tenderness, vagueness, candor, and abstraction.

Yes, I suppose you are. And yes, I was thinking of you. But of course I had to invent everything. I mean about the young man in my story. His background. His character. Everything. Naturally, I had no idea you were French. It was a pure coincidence.

You're right. It's quite an accident that we bumped into each other like that, and then again this afternoon in the French bookstore. I never thought we would meet again. Moinous squeezes his lips tight together and shakes his head several times in a gesture of total astonishment at his realization that such accidents can happen. Of course, he is not aware that he is suddenly entering the vain dream of love, the inexhaustible torrent of fair forms, the sterile and exquisite torture of understanding and loving.

I prefer to think of it as a coincidence, Sucette says, her voice taking on a somewhat philosophical tone, because, you see, an accident is just a thing that happens, whereas a coincidence is a thing that is going to happen and does.

Just like with us. Moinous cannot contain his happiness, though he is not sure he has understood the subtle distinction Sucette is making.

Yes, just like it happened with us. Sucette smiles. Perhaps we were destined to meet again, she says in a whisper, and then falls into silence, as if retreating into her own thoughts.

Moinous asks. What did you call me in your story?

Sucette hesitates. I invented a name. I called you Moinous. Well, that's what I call my French character.

Moinous? That's a funny name. I mean it's a nice name. It sounds French, but it's not a real name. Is it?

No, I made it up. I suppose it's obvious to you what it means. In fact, it's the heroine of my story who invents this name for the young Frenchman she meets on Washington Square. She says to him, after they fall in love, I'll call you Moinous to have a sense of togetherness with you.

Oh, I see. And they also meet on Washington Square, like us. This is really fabulous. Moinous? I like the name Moinous. Fits me well, don't you think?

Yes, it does. Sucette approves.

You know something, Moinous says after a moment of reflection, I just realized we haven't even introduced ourselves yet. But now you can call me Moinous. In fact, let's not ever tell each other our real names.

Then what will you call me? Sucette asks.

I don't know. Moinous brings his hand up to his mouth. Let me think. Let me think for a moment. And then he asks, What is the name of the girl in your story?

Susan. Susan Wakefield.

I got it, Moinous cries out joyfully. I'm going to call you Sucette.

Sucette? Why Sucette? What does it mean?

You know some French, don't you? *Une sucette* in French is a lollipop. It comes from the verb *sucer*. To suck.

Do I look like a lollipop to you? Sucette asks, unsure if Moinous is serious or joking.

No, it has nothing to do with looks. It's the first name that came to my mind when you said Susan. It's a nice sweet name. Don't you like it?

Oh, I think it's charming. No, really, I like it. It has a lovely sound to it. Especially when you say it. *Sucette.* Yes, I like it. SU-cette. Su-CETTE. She repeats the name several times, toying with the syllables, rolling them in her mouth like pieces of candy. Okay. You'll be Moinous and I'll be Sucette.

The two of them giggle as they repeat and connect each other's name, MOINOUS & SUCETTE, SUCETTE & MOINOUS, as if they have just invented each other on the spot.

You know what, Sucette says, still laughing, we should imagine nothing about ourselves beyond these two names. No past. No future.

Yes, yes nothing, nothing at all. Moinous agrees immediately, for he already knows that he is going to love Sucette in the light of the name he has just given her, just as Sucette already loves the Moinous she has created in her story. And certainly, for Moinous, all the delights of flesh and spirit will be contained in the name of Sucette, which he will repeat to himself time after time when he is alone, trying to kiss it with his lips whenever it passes through his mouth. And Sucette too will continue to murmur the name Moinous affectionately as she brings her story to its conclusion.

From the moment they talk to each other, Moinous & Sucette seem to be contained in their names, flesh, and spirit, with nothing beyond but the imaginary intensity and the fragile intangibility of their love story.

The waitress brings another cup of coffee. Are you sure you don't want anything with your coffee? Sucette asks again.

If you have a piece of pie, I'll have one too, Moinous says as if all such worldly decisions already rest with Sucette. The waitress smiles. Perhaps she's been listening to their conversation, enjoying from a privileged distance the tentative beginning of the love story of these two casual customers.

So tell me, Moinous asks, what happens in your story?

As they sip their second cups of coffee and eat the cheesecake they decided on, Sucette tells Moinous the story of Susan Wakefield. How she runs away from home because of her family's stifling Puritanism. She is the oldest daughter of a very wealthy and prominent Boston family. She comes to New York, penniless. At first she's very lost and lonely, but then she gets involved with politics, even though she knows nothing about it. Joins a Communist cell where she meets a young radical. His name is Tommy. He is an interesting character in the story. Very bright but very intense. He is black. Yes, a negro, from Chicago. Susan thinks she's in love with him. As you can see, it's a daring gesture of rebellion on her part against her family and her background. Things are sort of going well between Susan and Tommy. They spend long evenings together discussing Marxist ideology. During the day Susan works in a lampshade factory in Brooklyn. That's her assignment. While working she has to talk to the other workers and try to indoctrinate them into the Party. Then comes this big demonstration on Washington Square. One of the important scenes in the story. Against McCarthy. You know, the senator who's been accusing everybody of being a Communist, Sucette explains to Moinous as she brings a piece of cheesecake to her mouth with her fork. Susan is nervous about participating in this demonstration. It's the first time she's been involved in any kind of defying action against the government. But she's excited too. At the demonstration she bumps into a young man. The one who is somewhat modeled after you. The Frenchman I call Moinous. And she falls desperately in love with him. And of course, that really complicates the situation, because now Susan doesn't know how to tell Tommy. Sucette pauses to light a cigarette.

Sounds really interesting, Moinous comments. So, what you're in fact writing is a love story of sorts?

Yes, of course. But you must understand, Susan is very innocent about love, and about politics too. She has led a very sheltered life up to now. In fact, Tommy is the first man she has ever made love to. She's scared at first. She even says to him, when the intimate moment seems unavoidable, Perhaps we are too worldly for mere sexual pleasure. And indeed, she gives herself with such reserve and such contempt that Tommy is surprised at the quality of her eagerness. You see, Susan takes her pleasure not happily, but sadly and with Puritan guilt, because in spite of everything she cannot escape her background. I sort of like the way I wrote this, Sucette remarks as though speaking to herself, because it really defines Susan's character. She's a very complex person. She can be self-absorbed, self-indulgent, arrogant, and demanding, but she can also be sensible, thoughtful, generous, and likeable. Often she is many of these all at once. I worked very hard to try to capture Susan's personality. It's not easy, you know, to invent a credible character.

Is this story based on your own life? Moinous asks naively. I mean, did all these things happen to you too?

Well, not really. Susan is much younger than I am. Though, in a way, because I too come from Boston, you could say that Susan is a bit like me, and that we share some common traits. But I invented most of the details in the story.

I like this girl Susan, Moinous says. And then, after a slight pause, he asks Sucette, Does one learn a great deal about love while writing a love story?

Sucette replies that though love stories teach how to talk about love they do not necessarily teach how to make love. That's why Susan is so confused when she finally sleeps with Tommy. What she wants is a complete conjunction with him. A perfect balance. But she's unable to give herself completely. Maybe she's afraid of the consequences.

Oh, I see, Moinous says pensively. And then, abruptly, while blushing, perhaps realizing too late he should not ask this question, Does she find this balance with Moinous?

Sucette remains silent. She seems to be searching for an answer which cannot yet be articulated. Finally she says in a soft, evasive tone of voice, You know, most women are inadequate for the last merging.

And no doubt, when eventually Moinous & Sucette reach the fury of their conditional disappointment, all that will be left between them, besides the moisture of their bodies lost in the disorder of their nudity, will be the misunderstanding of their fragile relationship.

After a long moment of silence, Moinous asks, Are you also, like Susan, very political? When I first saw you, you seemed quite involved.

Sucette smiles enigmatically. Do you know the difference between involvement and commitment? I once heard a definition which I found very funny at the time, and yet very true. Think of ham and eggs.

Ham and eggs?

Yes, ham and eggs. Well, the chicken is involved, the pig is committed.

Oh, that's a good one. Moinous laughs, though he is not sure he has understood the difference. I suppose it's like being hungry and not being hungry, he says.

Well, not exactly, Sucette replies, puzzled by Moinous's lack of comprehension. She wonders if perhaps he has difficulties with the English language, though she finds his French accent charming and sexy.

You didn't answer my question about politics, Moinous says just to keep things going.

Oh, I'm less involved now. Especially since that day. I mean since the anti-McCarthy demonstration. It was such a mess. You know, with the police.

Yes, I know. I got hit on the head, Moinous says as he touches his left temple.

Oh my God, you were. I didn't even know that, Sucette exclaims with deep concern. I hope it wasn't serious.

No, it was nothing. Really nothing. Just a minor cut. Right here, Moinous points to his temple.

Oh, I'm glad. Sucette almost reaches across the table to touch Moinous's face. Instead she takes a sip of coffee from her cup. Yes, it was a strange afternoon. Something happened that day. I don't know what. But since that demonstration I've lost interest in politics completely. Especially the kind of politics I got caught up with. Maybe it's because I got so involved with this story. With Susan and. She stops. You know when you want to be a writer you have to sacrifice a great deal. I mean you have to be realistic about the choices you make. I suppose one could say I was too idealistic when it comes to politics, she murmurs, stressing the past tense just a touch, this being as close to regret as she can go.

Oh, I understand, Moinous says. So what happens in your story after Susan meets Moinous? Does she tell Tommy about it?

Well, it's much more complicated than that, you see, because at one point Susan discovers she's pregnant, but she's not sure if it's from Tommy or from the young Frenchman.

You mean Moinous?

Yes, Moinous. She decides to have an abortion without telling either of them, but she doesn't have the money because when she ran away from home she didn't want to have anything more to do with her family, and they in turn cut her off from all income. So she's trying to sell the little jewelry she has with her. These are old family heirlooms. So she feels guilty about it. But then, one evening, and that's really the climax of the story, as she sits in her room. She lives in a small furnished room near the Bowery. A cold-water flat. I mean really drab. She feels a tremendous pain in her body. She runs to the bathroom. It's a very cold and dreary evening. And there, all alone, twisting with pain, she has a miscarriage. It is as though all the confusion inside of her is coming out with the pain and the blood. It's very symbolic, of course.

Wow, this is getting better and better, Moinous says, all excited. Why can't I help? I mean, why can't the young Frenchman come in at this point and help her.

Well, that's one possibility. That's where I am now, in the story, and I'm not sure how to go on. I don't want to make it too sentimental. Too melodramatic. You understand what I mean. I don't know. I don't think I'm giving you the real sense of the situation. It's much deeper than that.

Oh no, I understand. Of course, it would be better if I could read the story myself to get the exact feel of it, Moinous says.

It would probably be a good place in the love story of Moinous & Sucette for her to suggest that perhaps they should go to her apartment where Sucette could then read her story to Moinous. Yes, Sucette could say, Look I don't want you to think I'm dragging you into something, but I really don't have anything to do this evening. How about you?

Me? Oh, I'm totally free.

Also, I don't want you to think that. I mean, I don't want you to get any ideas. Sucette blushes. That you and I are going to, you know. Or anything like that. But if you think it's all right, we can go to my apartment. I live on 105th Street. On the West Side. It's almost dinnertime. I can fix us something to eat and then, if you still feel like it, I'll read you my story.

Hey, that's a great idea, Moinous would answer. That's really fantastic. Yes, I would like very much to hear you read your story.

Honest? You mean it?

Yes I'm serious. Especially since I am in it. As he says this, a sensuous image flashes in Moinous's mind. He sees himself lying in Sucette's bed, his head resting on her naked bosom, her lovely hand caressing his back, her eyes darkening with fervor. She is whispering to him words that seem to fade into a sweet nonsense, she is saying, Let us love each other passionately since a stroke of luck has consigned us to this place. Then the image blurs and Sucette's voice vanishes as Moinous suddenly feels uneasy and apprehensive. He wonders now if Sucette is inviting him to go further than the reading of her story and mere conversation. He is happy enough to be sitting here with her talking like old friends. It has not occurred to him that perhaps that very evening he would already become intimate with Sucette. No he never imagined it would happen so quickly and so easily. He is not ready yet to verify the intensity of his desire. What sort of a woman is she? They hardly know each other. Moinous is filled with doubt and hesitancy.

Sucette is already standing, gathering her things, and insisting on paying for the coffee and the cheesecake. Their waitress smiles connivingly as she watches them leave Schrafft's.

After a short taxi ride, for which Sucette again insists on

paying, Moinous is sitting in a comfortable armchair in Sucette's apartment. He cannot believe he is here, here with her, and he doesn't even feel out of place. Sucette says, Make yourself at home, I'll be with you in a minute.

While she goes into the kitchen to prepare a light supper, as she puts it, Moinous examines the room.

He likes Sucette's apartment. It's almost the way he imagined it. One large, cozy room with an alcove at one end, where the bed is located. It's a huge bed, neatly made, with piles of colorful pillows casually thrown on it. A painting depicting two women sitting sideways on a terrace hangs on the wall behind the bed. Moinous thinks that the younger one looks a bit like Sucette. And the older one too. Perhaps it's a portrait of some of her relatives, though the costumes are very ancient. There are also two dogs in the painting. And two pigeons resting on the balustrade that surrounds the terrace. Moinous smiles as he remembers his friend Charlie, the one-legged pigeon. He does not realize that he is looking at a reproduction of "The Two Courtesans" by Carpaccio. The painting gives Moinous a warm feeling about Sucette, and also the plants he sees everywhere in the room, on the floor, in the windows, hanging from the ceiling, and the fresh flowers carefully arranged in a vase in the center of the table. Red tulips. Yes, it's a cozy apartment. One wall is covered with books, and there are more books on the table, on the chairs, on the floor. Moinous looks at the antique desk and imagines Sucette sitting there writing her story. He feels warm and happy, inside his bones.

Sucette has prepared a cheese omelette with French fries. She apologizes for not being able to do better, but of course she had not expected to have a guest for dinner. After the quick meal she reads her story to Moinous. She sits in her favorite armchair. Moinous is directly across from her in a rocking chair. There is a floor lamp between them which encloses them with its pale glow.

It's a good story. Even better than Sucette made it sound when she told him about it. Moinous, of course, particularly likes the passages where the young Frenchman is introduced into the plot. Yes, it's him. It could be him.

Sucette stops where Susan is having her miscarriage. That's as far as I am in the story, she says. As I told you, I don't know how to go on from here.

Though the story does not say so, Moinous asks if perhaps the miscarriage is self-induced.

I didn't think of that, Sucette says with an equivocal look on her face. But then, after a brief moment of reflection. No. Absolutely not. It would be totally out of character for Susan to do a thing like that.

Moinous & Sucette continue to discuss the story. Susan's personality. Tommy's idealism, and his anger when he finds out about the young man Susan is now involved with. Moinous thinks that the love scenes between Susan and Moinous are really well written, and very touching. The whole story, in fact, is extremely well done. But they cannot think of an ending for it.

That's still the one big problem I have, Sucette says. I cannot think of a way to end the story.

Moinous jokingly suggests a double suicide. They both

laugh as they dismiss this possibility. Too melodramatic. Suddenly Sucette yawns. Oh excuse me, she says. She looks at her watch. Oh my God, it's already two-thirty. I didn't realize it was that late. We've been sitting here talking all this time. I'm exhausted. Aren't you? It's been a long day, a very exciting day, but I think you better go now. It's so late, and I have so many things to do tomorrow. I must get up early.

Moinous doesn't know what to say. By now he had assumed . . . He had expected more, even though earlier he felt apprehensive about coming to Sucette's apartment and confronting the possibility of . . . of having to make love to her. He glances toward the alcove as if suggesting something. But Sucette is already handing him his jacket and leading him to the door.

You must go now, she says in a firm voice. You will call me, won't you? Oh I almost forgot. Here, I'll give you my telephone number. She writes it on a piece of paper. You promise?

A moment later Moinous is walking alone in the deserted street. He turns onto West End Avenue. The wind blows cold rain in his face, and he shivers. He is totally confused. Baffled even. He doesn't know if he should feel happy or tortured.

Of course, Moinous is unaware that this is the beginning of forty-two days of frustration. Yes, unaware that for the next forty-two days Sucette is going to keep him at bay and refuse to surrender to the physical pleasures of love, and that he will be wandering in the streets of New York like a mad dog, his body aching with the pains of desire and the throbbings of wasted hope.

Sometimes he walks as far down as Washington Square after he leaves Sucette's apartment in the middle of the night, just to empty his heart to Charlie, the one-legged pigeon, telling him how he cannot understand what's going on. She keeps asking me to come over to her place. We talk for hours. It's really beautiful. We discuss all sorts of things. She wants to know everything about my life. We seem so happy together. She even lets me kiss her. Touch her. But when the time comes, you know what I mean, she simply pushes me away. I don't understand. Maybe there's something wrong with me. She keeps saying to me, One must have principles in matters of love.

During these forty-two days of rejection, Moinous is unable to keep his equilibrium. He discovers that he cannot even sublimate the deep and constant pain and rage of his frustration into irony or vengeful laughter. He tries every approach to convince Sucette to give in. He begs. He cries. Whines. Screams. He even goes so far as to say that he will kill himself if she does not let him make love to her. Sucette is unmovable. Of course, Moinous does not realize that one always thinks the act of dying will punish the lover when actually it frees her. Nor does he understand that sexual difference is not a bodily fact, but the arbitrary product of a shared social code.

As time passes, everything gradually seems to go wrong for him. Even his job at the cafeteria is falling apart. Moinous has been dropping so many dishes lately that his boss tells him, Look, Frenchy, you break one more dish in that kitchen of mine and you're out. I can't afford you anymore. That's all Moinous needs now. To find himself without a job again. And even Joseph, his

Armenian friend, is turning into a selfish wise-ass. And on top of that the heat in Moinous's room on 23rd Street is not working properly. The furnace blows up in the basement of the building, and the owner is stalling about getting it replaced. When it rains for Moinous, it's always a deluge.

Meanwhile Sucette struggles to bring Susan's story to an end. She cannot find the right words, the right aggregate of words to conclude her love story. And so, she makes Moinous suffer forty-two days of humiliation and despair. Forty-two days of vain desire and unfulfilled hope, which may be wasted unless Sucette finishes her story. And of course, remain hypothetical unless Moinous & Sucette meet again beyond the exchange of smiles on Washington Square.

And even if Moinous & Sucette were to meet again, at the Librairie Française, or some other place in the city, and play out the scenario of their love story. Go for coffee together, and so on. It is quite probable that things would not work out for them in the long run. Or at least not for Moinous, whose luck always runs out too soon.

For instance, as Moinous & Sucette sit at Schrafft's, talking like old friends, a young man would probably appear on the scene. An elegant young man wearing a Brooks Brothers Harris tweed with gray flannel pants, button-down collar, striped tie, his blondish hair neatly parted on the side, and Sucette would say, Oh, there you are Richard, as if expecting him all the while. And as this young man takes Sucette's hand to lead her away, she would say to Moinous, Well, it was nice talking to you. Perhaps we'll meet again. And poor Moinous would sit there, crushed by his own insecurity, thrown back where he belongs, in the mud of despair and loneliness, having to endure again the miserable hope of wanting to be loved, wishing he had never seen this charming blonde on Washington Square, and never smiled at her.

Raymond Federman was born in Paris, France, in 1928, and came to the U.S. in 1947. He writes both in English and in French, and sometimes translates his own work from one language to the other. During the 1950s, he lived in New York City where he studied at Columbia University, then in California where he received his Ph.D. at U.C.L.A. Aside from having published two books on the work of Samuel Beckett, and two volumes of poems, he is the author of five novels—*Double or Nothing* (winner of the Frances Steloff Fiction Prize), *Amer Eldorado, Take It or Leave It, The Voice in the Closet,* and *The Twofold Vibration.* A Guggenheim Fellow in 1966, a Fulbright recipient in 1982, he was awarded a National Endowment for the Arts Fellowship in creative writing for 1985. He currently lives in Buffalo where he is Professor of English and Comparative Literature at SUNY/Buffalo, as well as Director of the Creative Writing Program.

The Red Menace, Michael Anania

Inherit the Blood, Barney Bush

Coagulations, Jayne Cortez

To Those Who Have Gone Home Tired, W.D. Ehrhart

She Had Some Horses, Joy Harjo

Dos Indios, Harold Jaffe

Living Room, June Jordan

America Made Me, Hans Koning

Mozart, Westmoreland and Me, Marilyn Krysl

When the Revolution Really, Peter Michelson

Echoes Inside the Labyrinth, Thomas McGrath

Fightin', Simon Ortiz

From Sand Creek, Simon Ortiz

Saturday Night at San Marcos, William Packard

The Mojo Hands Call/I Must Go, Sterling Plumpp

Somehow We Survive, Sterling Plumpp

Homegirls & Handgrenades, Sonia Sanchez

The Man Who Cried I Am, John A. Williams